A Jenny-Dog and the Son of Light Novel

# CODY

# D.M. GREENWALD

DENVER, COLORADO

Outskirts Press, Inc.
http://www.outskirtspress.com

Paperback ISBN: 978-1-4787-3398-0
Hardback ISBN: 978-1-4787-3409-3

Outskirts Press and the "OP" logo are trademarks belonging to Outskirts Press, Inc.

PRINTED IN THE UNITED STATES OF AMERICA

*There are three things necessary for a fire, any fire, to occur: flammable material, oxygen, and temperature above the point of ignition. During dry years in high mountain forests the first two elements are always present. Lightning completes the triangle which can be rejuvenating or devastating. Sometimes it is both.*

# Prologue

*9:00 p.m.*
*Friday, August 25, 1972*
*Shoshone National Forest, Wyoming*

    *For Travis and Macauley, the night comes on with no perceptible difference other than thicker smoke and higher winds. The fires have grown to over seven thousand acres and are spreading fast in three directions. Laura Miller is in sporadic radio contact with the fire crews via the spotter plane. Arthur Marshall searches his maps and his mind for another place to try to make a stand.*

    *The firefighters work feverishly digging and scraping and raking the four foot wide trench down to mineral soil; praying against all evidence and experience that the fire-line will hold.*

    *Sheriff Dugan and Hank Thurston head back to the campsite, worried and disappointed and pretty sure they are going the right way.*

    *Guy Macauley and Joshua Travis and the dogs bang down the Muddy Creek trail in Miller's Forestry Service jeep. Joshua tries to take note of direction and landmarks, but it's too damn dark to see much of anything despite the ominous glow in the distance. He wonders how Macauley knows where the hell they are going.*

    *Three miles and fifteen minutes later they are on foot, having gone as far as possible in the jeep.*

*Dr. Carolyn Barstow sits alone in a corner of the lookout station, waiting and crying and praying.*

*Kristian lights another cigarette and has another drink.*

*The good people of Cody, Wyoming and Red Lodge, Montana look out their windows at that same glow in the distance. They are worried about the direction of the fires and their loved ones on the line as they tuck their children into bed and kiss them goodnight.*

*And two teenagers and their father are out in that dangerous night, lost as hell.*

# Chapter One

*February, 1978*
*Lincoln County, Wisconsin*

It was cold and lonely when Joshua Travis finally got home from work. The dogs and the horses were making a row. The snow and the wind had eased. An occasional patch of black sky and a lonely star or two revealed themselves for the first time in three days.

Joshua carried the supplies inside the mud room, started a fire in the old wood burner in the kitchen, and put on a pot of coffee. Then he went back outside to feed the animals and take care of the chores. It was almost nine o'clock before he finally got to rustle up some food for himself. By the time Joshua got through eating and washing up the dishes it was nearly quarter to ten.

The big man started bringing the supplies in from the mud room. Best to get things squared away before hitting the hay. But he could see the lights of a car coming up the drive. That took him by surprise. As it approached, Joshua saw it was a sheriff's cruiser. His focus narrowed keenly. He could feel his heart pounding. *Lord, don't have him ask me to go out again tonight.*

"Kris!" Maureen Andersen called out from her booth. It was wet and dreary in San Francisco. Cronin's was one of the oldest taverns in town. Black walnut woodwork and polished brass rails and counters illuminated by harsh incandescent overhead lights combined to make the establishment at once harshly bright and warmly cozy. It smelled of cigarette smoke and beer. Had it been any night other than Monday, the bar and restaurant would have been packed. As it was, the writer had had no trouble getting a table. The two women hugged briefly. Andersen was a tall stunning redhead with skin so white it was almost translucent. Kristian was also tall, but she was a blond with classic features and a figure that made men ache. Both women were in their thirties. Andersen looked at her friend, shook her head, and smiled. "Well, he did it, didn't he?"

Kristian smiled and nodded as they sat down. "Yes, he did."

"So...? Have you spoken to him?"

Kristian looked up, surprised by the question, not knowing why she was surprised. "As a matter of fact I have. I called him last night." For the first time in over three years, she did not add.

"And...?"

"And what?"

Andersen just cocked her head and waited.

"He sounded tired. And maybe a little sad."

"Sad? Why in the world was he sad? My God, he saved that little girl, didn't he? I checked with the Free Press in Burlington. They said she's doing fine. Won't have to lose any toes or anything."

Kristian nodded, happy for the child. "I don't know. Maybe it was my imagination. It was pretty late. Maybe he was just tired or drained." She had that part right.

"Did he talk about the rescue?"

"Not much. He just said that things were cut pretty close." Kristian looked across the table at Maureen. "When Joshua says things were cut pretty close, it means that they almost died."

Now it was Andersen's turn to stare. "Wow," was all she was able to murmur. Everyone she had spoken to in Vermont, and elsewhere, had said that the whole thing was just one big miracle.

Their middle-aged waiter appeared, white apron over black trousers and shoes, white shirt, sleeves rolled up, no tie, no pad.

"Ladies..."

"Hi, Jim," Kristian smiled.

"Something from the bar?"

"Just coffee for me," Andersen ordered.

"I'll have the same, Jim." Kristian had just come off the longest weekend of her life. Almost as long as the night of the fire. She had gotten through it with the help of friends, prescription drugs and alcohol. Now she was straight, and she needed to stay that way. "You wouldn't happen to have any corned-beef and cabbage left over, would you?"

"I can check, Kris. And for you, miss?"

Maureen Andersen looked over the menu. She was glad that Kristian had ordered a dinner. It meant that she was in no hurry. "How's the orange roughy?"

The waiter shook his head. "The salmon is better."

Andersen smiled and nodded. "That'll be fine."


Joshua watched Jonathan VanStavern get out of the car and trudge the short distance to the house. He met him with an open door and a wary look, relieved to learn that the visit was a social one and that there wasn't another kid or someone lost that he had to go look for.

"Come on in, Jon. There's coffee on the stove. Help yourself."

"You need a hand?"

"Naw. I'm just storing away some supplies and repacking my winter pack. Had to get a new rig, you know. What do you think?" It was another big Jansport. VanStavern squatted down, examined it closely then hefted it up by the strap to one shoulder.

"Looks like it oughta do the trick. Ah, listen, Josh, I know you lost a lot of gear. You send any bills for new equipment you need over to my office, you hear?"

"Sure thing, Jon, but I'll have to send you copies. I've already been told to send the bills to the ski lodge, the sheriff out in Vermont, and to Kelly's parents. I'm looking to make out like a bandit."

VanStavern didn't give a shit if Joshua Travis became a millionaire. He would still pay gladly.

"Margaret and I have been trying to get a hold of you all day, but I didn't want Emily using the emergency band. We wanted to have you over for supper."

"I appreciate that, Jonathan. That would have been nice. And I appreciate you not using the emergency band. It was a real bitch out there today. Damn barn was a real bear. Built on a knoll, oh, maybe eighty, a hundred years ago. Just didn't want to come down. Didn't matter where we positioned the vehicles, they kept slipping and sliding in the snow."

"You have chains on?" VanStavern smiled to himself, knowing full well that he surely had, and not a little amazed that his friend had made it to work at all.

"Sure thing. After lunch it was coming down pretty hard, so we had to finish what we started."

VanStavern nodded. Joshua wouldn't leave an unstable structure standing, and once the barn was down they wouldn't be able to leave the lumber just piled up on the ground. There'd be no telling when they might dig it out. "So you took it apart and loaded it all on the flatbed?"

"Afraid so. We didn't get done 'til after six. Didn't get back to the yard 'til around eight. I guess that's why I missed your message. Emily was long gone." Joshua smiled. "We earned our money today. I told the boys they could have tomorrow off."

Jonathan VanStavern just shook his head. Joshua finished putting away the last few things in the den. He came back into the kitchen carrying two bottles, Wild Turkey for the sheriff, Canadian Club for himself. Jonathan nodded. Joshua poured three fingers of each. He stoked the fire and sat down at the table with his old friend.

"To you and the dogs," Jonathan raised his glass.

"To the dogs." They touched glasses. "And the Air National Guard. That was some crew you found me."

VanStavern grinned. "I thought they might be."

"Real maniacs. I never would have gotten in if it hadn't been for them."

VanStavern nodded.

"And I surely appreciate you picking us up in Madison last night, Jon."

"Hell, that was the least I could do."

Joshua hesitated. "Did I tell you Kristian called last night or this morning or whenever the hell it was that you dropped me off?"

Jonathan VanStavern took a long drink of Bourbon.

Outside, the San Francisco night was cold and wet and dark. Inside the Irish tavern the lights blazed invitingly.

"He must have thought I was crazy, Mo, calling him like that, but I just couldn't help myself. I just had to talk to him."

The writer nodded. "Sure, Kris." Their coffee came.

"It's funny, you know, after all that's happened. I used to spend an ungodly amount of energy looking for chinks in Joshua's armor, especially when we first started dating. But after Cody I realized that he didn't have any armor, and I knew that this time he would either come back with that kid alive, or he wouldn't come back at all."

Andersen was reluctant to interrupt, but she did. "Hold on, Kris. You're losing me."

"Sorry. I spent most of the weekend with Jane Sloan, and she knows most of this."

"How is Jane?"

"Pregnant."

"You're kidding. Jane?"

Kristian smiled and nodded. "She's down in Acapulco right now, covering some fashion show."

"Good for her."

"You don't know the half of it." Kristian laughed.

"So who or what was Cody, Kris? And what do you mean that you realized Joshua didn't have any armor? I take it that's some kind of metaphor?"

"Cody is this town in Wyoming, out near Yellowstone. Joshua and the dogs were called in to look for some people lost in the Beartooth Mountains. But there was this fire," Kristian hesitated. She began to choke up. "Things didn't go well."

Andersen stared at her friend, deciding how to best proceed.

"Look, Kris, why don't you start from the beginning. Same ground rules as before, no recorder, no notes. I have all night if you do."

Kristian knew this was where she was heading. It was why she had agreed to meet Andersen again. She needed an objective ear to help her consider and evaluate her thoughts. Who better than Maureen? She would have to be careful, especially now. But this was what she wanted.

"You've got to swear to me that you won't write anything about Joshua without clearing it with us first, Mo. Not even fiction."

Andersen considered the terms. It wasn't even close. What the hell, she decided, if the rest of this story was anything like the part she had already heard, she wouldn't miss it for the world. "You have my word, Kris. I swear."

"It's getting late, Josh. I'd better mosey on home." Sheriff VanStavern stood up.

"How about one more for the road, Jon?" Joshua reached for the bottle of Bourbon. VanStavern covered his glass with his large hand. But he sat back down.

"Any more of that stuff and I'll have to arrest myself for D.W.I. But maybe another cup of coffee." He suspected his friend could use some company, late as it was.

Joshua lifted the coffeepot from the wood burner and poured. He poured a cup for himself too.

"You know, Josh, when you first brought Kristian home, nobody around here thought she would last a year. In fact, nobody thought she would last one winter. Hell, they were making book on it down at the Blazer."

Joshua smiled. "I might have taken some of that action myself, Jon. Funny how things work out, isn't it."

"Yeah," VanStavern frowned, "funny."

*Midnight*
*August 25, 1972*
*Shongopovi pueblo*
*Tusayan Plateau, Arizona*


*The black, star-filled sky envelops the sleeping village.  Blue Corn Woman leaves her bed and climbs the ladder to the roof of her pueblo. Little Sooki, her granddaughter, follows silently. The old woman pauses on the roof, then faces north. Sooki watches from the top of the ladder. She is puzzled. She cannot see the flashes of lightning the old woman sees a thousand miles away. She does not hear the rolling thunder. After much time has passed, Sooki hears her grandmother utter one word:*

Topqolu, *Hell.*

# Chapter Two

*3:30 a.m.*
*Friday, August 25, 1972*
*Clay Butte, Wyoming*

*From the third story of the recently decommissioned lookout tower, Richie Volas watches the flashing heat lightning and occasional crackling grounded ribbon-bolt. He has been doing so since about midnight. This time it seems different. He hesitates. After all, he is only a summer temp in between college semesters. Then he makes the call to his supervisor.*

*"Uh, Mr. Thurston, I'm sorry to bother you, but there was just one heck of a lightning strike northwest of here, probably up around Thiel Lake, I'm guessing. Can't say for sure if there's a fire, but this one seemed different. Maybe a little after-glow. I don't know, maybe it's just my eyes."*

*"Okay, son, you did the right thing. That's why I put you out there."*

*Thurston is old school. Commissioned or decommissioned, Clay Butte still has a tower and the supervising ranger of the Shoshone National forests wants his new people to experience watchtower duty. Especially during a summer like this one.*

*"I don't suppose you got any rain with that lightning?"*

*"Not here. Can't say about the north."*

*"Which way is the wind coming from?"*

*Volas has to turn on the spotlight to view the windsock.*

*"Looks to be about southwest." (A good thing.)*

*"Okay now, Ritchie, here's what we're going to do. I'll call Art Marshall up in Missoula and try to line up some jump teams for first light. I'll also call Red Lodge. You keep a lookout and map any suspicious strikes. Call me every hour."*

*"Yes sir."*

*"You did the right thing, Richie. With any luck, the wind will keep things north of the line."*

*The big, fifty-year-old supervising ranger knows better than to count on luck.*

The snow was picking up again outside the Travis homestead, but inside it was warm and toasty. Joshua's muscles were stiff and sore as he moved around his kitchen and his pantry. He probably should have taken the day off; he had certainly earned it. But, despite his aches and pains, Joshua felt pretty good. He was happy that VanStavern wasn't asking him to go out again, at least not that night, and he was happy to have a good friend with whom he could talk and tell stories and hash things out. Most of all, he was happy about how this last rescue had gone, close as it had been. Joshua and the child he had saved were lucky to be alive, much more than lucky, he knew. And he was happy that he *knew* they were lucky to be alive. That hadn't been the case five-and-a-half years ago after the disastrous Cody operation and its aftermath. And Joshua Paul Travis had never forgiven himself.

The rain outside Cronin's Tavern intermittently increased and then eased, typical San Francisco winter weather of drizzle and fog punctuated by squalls blown in from the ocean or the bay.

"This salmon is really good," Anderson remarked. "Remind me

to leave a nice tip for the waiter."

"Jim's a nice guy." Despite the special order, Kristian only picked at the massive Irish dinner heaped on her plate. Even on a hungry night she would have only made a dent in the generous piles of boiled beef, cabbage, salt potatoes and carrots. Still, it was nice just sitting in the cozy old tavern, looking out at the dark wet streets and losing yourself in the multi-colored lights reflected and refracted by the rain. "You know, it's funny how you remember things. You know what I mean…? I mean, you don't necessarily remember things rationally or even chronologically, but more emotionally and almost at random."

"Like how?"

"Well, like the thing I remember best about Joshua was the way he used to read to me."

"He used to read to you?"

Kristian nodded. "Each month on the first or second day, no later than the third unless he was away, Joshua would read to me the appropriate chapter of Aldo Leopold's *Sand County Almanac*."

"He's the one you told me about the other night."

"That's right. In the winter Joshua would read to me by the fire or by the stove in the kitchen, over pie and coffee after dinner. In the spring it might be on a dreary April morning listening to the rain against the roof and the windows. And in summer it would usually be out on the porch at dusk, the evening before I knew he was going to drag me out of bed at some ungodly hour to show me something the next day."

"Show you something like what?"

"Oh some dramatic little story written in feathers and blood alongside one of the paths in the woods. Or maybe some pink or blue wild flower just coming into bloom that was mentioned in Leopold's monthly chronicle."

The freelance writer shook her head and smiled.

"Joshua really loves his home and the land and forests around it in Lincoln County. And the people of Lincoln County really love him. They love him so much that they even forgave him for not going on to play football at the University of Wisconsin and fulfilling their dream of having a local boy star for the Green Bay Packers."

"Was he really that good?"

Kristian looked up. "There's this bar and restaurant called the Blazer Pub, on the way into Merrill. Kind of like this place only cozier, more country, with a nice warm fieldstone fireplace and a horseshoe bar where they would buy you a third drink for every two that you ordered. And you know, Mo, after almost twenty years they were still showing the old game films of the 1954 and 1955 State Championship games that Josh had starred in."

"Really?"

"Really. Oh, he tried to credit the team and the coaching and even the fans, but you didn't have to be a football aficionado to see that one player was clearly the star in both games... And that makes me think back to the first time we went to the beach together while we were still in California, just a couple of weeks after we first met, and how I couldn't believe how beautiful he was or how good he made me feel. And now I wonder why I ever thought the crazy things I thought and pulled the foolish stunts that I tried, usually only to have them backfire. But of course I know. I always did know."

Maureen Andersen was puzzled. She knew Joshua Travis was tall and good-looking. She had pulled the old files and photos over the weekend. Still, she did not know what Kristian was driving at. She said nothing.

"Was the corned beef and cabbage all right, Kris?" The waiter asked. Kristian had hardly touched her food.

"It was fine, Jim. I'm just not very hungry."

"How was your salmon, miss?"

"It was a good choice. Thank you for suggesting it."

"Anything for dessert? We still have some cheesecake from Corsigllia's."

Kristian smiled. "Just some more coffee for me. Bring her a piece of the cheesecake."

"Thanks a lot."

"And two forks," Kristian conceded as the waiter turned to the kitchen.

"This story gets more unbelievable by the minute. It's almost as good as your Indian story."

"And I guess that brings me right back to the very beginning, or at least the beginning of our relationship, on a sunny Monday morning in June of 1967. Were you here then?"

"I was still in Boston, at B.U."

"You missed a real trip. San Francisco in the summer of '67 was The City of Light. It was like the reluctant Mecca of a young generation, and we were all so damn sure we were embarking upon the new cultural, political, social, and economic renaissance of the Western World. Amazing hubris, now that I look back, but back then it was a city in which anything and everything could and would be found, from Osley acid to motorcycle Zen. Christ, if it was new or exciting, it was here."

Andersen smiled and nodded.

"But also here, in peaceful if not always accepting coexistence, was the traditional old town of hills and Victorian homes and Fisherman's Wharf and gray stone apartments and white stucco houses and, of course, the cable cars and the gardens and the beautiful bridges. And standing like a bastion in the center of it all was the San Francisco of steel and glass and concrete, the San Francisco of trade and commerce and business and even art. And it was in this San Francisco that I met Joshua Paul Travis on a day I will never forget as long as I live." Kristian sipped her coffee, losing herself in her memories, wondering why her coffee wasn't something stronger.

Andersen waited patiently. Her silence encouraged Kristian to continue.

"I was walking to work as usual that morning except that Jane wasn't with me. It was a beautiful June morning, and she had taken off for Stinson beach."

"Sounds like Jane."

Now Kristian smiled and nodded. "We had made it a point to keep to our same route and routine despite the construction and the construction workers that had been there for about a month, and I used to tell myself that being an architect gave me a legitimate reason for walking that close to the building site. But, of course, once we stepped onto the plywood walkway that went past the plywood fence surrounding the foundation excavations, we always kept our eyes straight ahead and did our best to tune out the cat calls and lewd whistles that came from the hard-hats at the site. You know how it is."

Andersen did. Like Kristian, she was a beautiful woman. "Maybe you did. If I know Sloan, she whistled back and shouted things that would make the hard-hats blush. You were probably just too busy tuning things out to notice."

"Well, I must have been doing a damn good job of it that day because I sure as hell would have walked into that dump truck that came roaring out from the break in the plywood fence had it not been for someone grabbing my arm and pulling me back out of the way."

"You're kidding."

Kristian shook her head. "And I don't mind telling you, Mo, he could have had me right then and there, if he had asked, and that was *before* I even realized what he looked like."

"Jesus, Kris, he probably could have had me under *those* circumstances."

Kristian smiled again. She had recently learned that her friend preferred women. "In fact, Mo, I was too damn shaken to pay any attention to, much less care, what anybody looked like at the time. All I remembered was that he was really tall and he felt very strong, and, for some crazy reason, I remembered that he had a hammer hanging from a metal loop on his belt. But do you want to know the thing I remembered the best and still do remember to this day?"

Andersen waited.

"It was how he didn't chastise me or even tell me to watch out. He just looked at me and asked in a very sincere, almost gentle way, if I was all right. And when I nodded and said, *yes, thank you*, he just nodded and said, *take it easy*, in a kind voice as he let go of my arm and went back to work."

"Jesus, Kris," Maureen was beginning to feel the same magical entrancement that she had experienced the other night when Kristian, scared to death about Joshua's safety, had shared other intimate aspects of this man.

"Talk about getting blown over, Maureen, I just couldn't get over that morning."

"I can see why. I mean, Christ, you nearly got killed."

"I don't mean the part about almost getting run down by a stupid dump truck. I shook that off by the time the 10:30 coffee break rolled along. But the part about this clean cut, Gary Cooper type hard-hat casually saving my life and then just politely asking about my welfare, without putting any moves on me or even trying to cop a feel... Well, that was too much like something out of a story book for me to handle, and it made me pretty useless the rest of the day."

*She goes back to the construction site early the next morning, dressed to kill and braving the hoots and leers of the workers, so that she can give him one red rose that she has bought from a street vendor on Union St. He looks into her eyes and just easily says thank you as she hands the flower to him.*

*She keeps going by early each morning that week, usually seeing him and smiling or saying good morning, until finally on Friday he asks her if she might care to have dinner with him and perhaps show him a little of San Francisco. She says sure and figures that now she has her chance to even the score.*

"...And that was the way I met Kristian, Jon. After almost getting run down by a cement mixer that was barreling out of the job site the day before, she just came back the next day, bold as brass, and, saying she just wanted to thank me again, she handed me one red rose. I surely was impressed, I can tell you, by how gutsy she was, walking onto that construction job like that, what with all the guys staring and grinning and calling out things to her. And she sure was a good looking gal. Downright beautiful was what she was. Hell, you know that. But the thing that stuck with me throughout the rest of the day was something that I couldn't quite put my finger on. Something I thought maybe I saw in her eyes or her mouth or somewhere in her face that most people weren't aware of but that seemed to tell me that despite her smiling, attractive, self-confident appearance, she maybe wasn't quite as happy as she ought to be and that she was maybe a little more vulnerable than she liked to let on."

*That about summed it up,* VanStavern knew.

"I knew that this was one woman that I should probably let pass... but that I probably wouldn't."

"It was funny, Mo, no, actually, I guess it was sick, but it wasn't that I especially wanted to go out with some hard-hat, or that I felt that I owed him anything," Kristian looked towards her friend, "although I figured that *he* probably thought I owed him something.

"But what I really wanted to do was to show him, and I suppose myself, that I could be as cool and as poised as any man. This whole business had really messed up my mind, and I thought that by seeing

him again and giving him the rose, I would dispel the Gary Cooper/
White Knight image I had carried around with me the day before
and that I knew had to be wrong for sure. But of course it didn't
work because, in the first place, he wasn't trying to prove anything
to anybody. And, in the second place, he actually was like that and
then some."

*They're pouring concrete on Friday so he's late getting off work and he
has to hustle to make their seven-thirty date. He's wearing a shirt and tie,
with gray slacks and desert boots, and he's carrying a navy blue blazer, the
only sport coat he owns, over his right arm. He bounces up the steps of the
old Victorian house on Green Street like some handsome college athlete.*

"I can still remember it like it was yesterday, Jon. Kristian was
wearing this light, cream colored dress that you could, ah, sort of see
through when the light was right, with a brightly colored scarf on
her neck." *And no bra*, he doesn't tell his friend. "She was absolutely
stunning, and men kept eyeing her all night no matter where we
went.

"She took me to this little inexpensive French place, over by
Presidio Heights, that she had discovered a year before and that was
just starting to catch on. She knew the owner and the waiter, and
they made a big fuss over her and over us, giving us their best table
by the window. I was real impressed, and I got to chatting a little
with the owner. It turned out that he wasn't really French. But he
was *Quebecois*, from Sherbrooke, and we talked a little about places
we both knew."

"And so there I was," Kristian continued, "trying to show this guy
how *in* and sophisticated I was with my few words of French and
kisses on the cheeks and all, in a restaurant that definitely did not
cater to a hard-hat clientele. And there he was, rattling off French

like a native and talking about old times with the owner like they were long lost cousins."

Maureen Andersen laughed. "Serves you right."

Kristian nodded. "That was how I found out a little bit about his background and that his mother was French Canadian and had died when he was in high school. I don't think he would have volunteered it otherwise. It was just one of the many surprises that I had in store for me, and not just during the beginning either."

"Like what?"

"Well, for instance, I couldn't believe it when I found out he was over thirty. I would have guessed early twenties from the way he looked and carried himself, and having just turned twenty-three myself, thirty seemed quite distant, especially back then when we weren't supposed to trust anyone over that age."

Andersen knew Kristian's age and professional background. She did the math on Joshua.

"I've often wondered if I would have kept seeing him if I had found out his age that first night. But, as I said, he didn't volunteer much, or perhaps I didn't give him much of a chance between the whirlwind bus and cable-car tour I was giving him and trying to impress the hell out of him with my own sophistication and accomplishments."

"Kristian was exciting to be with on that first night, Jon. She's the type of person that gives her undivided attention to anything she is interested in or focused on. And she really knows San Francisco well, especially the buildings but also a lot of its history, and going around with Kris was like being taken on a private tour with one exceptionally well informed (and classy looking) tour-guide. We finally wound up down by Fisherman's Wharf, and, after walking along the docks and looking at boats and chatting with some of the fishermen for a bit, she brought me to a diner. The place was called the Buena Vista Cafe, down near the cable-car turnaround. I guess it's pretty well known in certain circles; lots of pictures of famous people on the walls. And besides being a diner, it was also a bar and a coffee house to boot. The place was crowded and jumping, and it seemed like half the people there knew Kristian. Well, half the guys anyway."

*At the Buena Vista, Kristian is really in her element...* "...but I knew that I had to be careful who we wound up talking to because a lot of the people there were just regular blue-collar workers, and I still wanted to see Joshua uncomfortable so that I could come to *his* rescue or some such thing. Though I must admit that by midnight this idea was receding farther and farther to the back of my mind. We wound up next to some university types that I knew, art-history professors and literature grad students and the like, and they were talking about books and art and the theatre and such, and I thought that they ought to do just fine. But it surprised me to see how easily Joshua fit in. Not because he was like them, because he wasn't, but because he didn't try to be like them. He just showed a sincere interest in what they were discussing and occasionally asked a more relevant question than one would have expected from a construction worker.

"It had been the same earlier, when I was showing him around town a little. He was just like a kid. Happy to see anything and interested in everything. He didn't try to act blasé about things, and he didn't try to not act like a tourist. He was just happy to be seeing things and doing things and, it seemed, to be with me. And while he did take my hand or my arm at times, and he casually touched my shoulder or my back on occasion, he didn't try to use some romantic view or secluded spot to slip his arm around me or to try to kiss me. And damn if I wasn't beginning to relax and enjoy being with him in spite of my original intentions. It was also becoming very apparent that this guy was quite different from what I had expected him to be."

*I'll say*, Andersen thought to herself.

"When the group we were with found out that he was a hard-hat they sort of raised their eyebrows, and some of them tried to make him look small in front of me by asking him how he felt about the war, figuring that he would be for it and then they could proceed to lecture him on the errors of his ways. They also talked about the recent production of *Il Trovatore* that was being performed to much acclaim at the Opera House, and they asked him if he had seen it yet."

"How did he handle that?"

Kristian smiled. "He told them that he was against the war but probably not for the same reasons that they were. As far as the opera was concerned, he just told them no, he hadn't seen that production. Of course one smart ass then asked him just which production he *had* seen."

"And?"

"Josh just casually said, *the one at La Scalla back in 1960,* and we left them with their mouths open as we moved across the crowded smoke filled room towards an exit."

"You've got to be shitting me," Andersen said, her own mouth wide open.

Kristian just nodded, smiling. "As we were leaving, Joshua whispered in my ear, *Do you think I should tell them that I was bored stiff during most of it and that I almost fell asleep during the second act?* And I looked up and kissed him on the cheek. And I remember how he beamed."

*Masauwu, the Skeleton Man, was the Spirit of Death and the Keeper of Fire. He was chosen to test the pahana and see if he was really the Son of Light.*

*The first lightning strike hit a one hundred-and-fifty-year-old lodgepole pine northwest of Thiel Lake. Sixty million volts crackled and swirled down the length of the tree to the ground, igniting dead pine cones, needles, and debris on the forest floor with a flash. More slowly, almost deliberately, the flames worked their way around the trunk and back up the seventy-foot tree to its drought parched crown. It immediately burst into flames, embers popping in all directions. Within minutes, the first quarter-acre of the Absaroka Beartooth Wilderness in the Gallatin National Forest was on fire.*

# Chapter Three

*3:40 a.m.*
*August 25, 1972*
*Crandall, Wyoming*

*Hank Thurston calls Arthur Marshall, Region One Fire Supervisor, in Missoula Montana. Marshall is not pleased to get the call. Won't this summer ever end, he thinks to himself.*

*"I wish I could tell you more, Arthur, but right now that's all we know. Figured you would want a heads up."*

*Marshall flips through his log book and assorted notes posted on his nightstand. "Only have one team of jumpers on base at the moment, and they've only been off the line for a few days. I'll work on scrounging up some additional crews wherever I can find them. We'll need a lot more than one team if things really get going. Know where you want them?"*

*"Not yet. I'll try to get Mitch Walker to take a look soon as it's light."*

*"You know I'll catch hell if we jump into a wilderness area."*

*"Not asking you to, Arthur. Just want to make sure things stay north of the line, if possible."*

*"We'll do our best, Hank. That's all I can promise."*

*Hank Thurston is satisfied. He knows Arthur Marshall well. Still, he has a nagging fear in his gut. He is old enough to remember the Crandall Creek fire back in '35. And he was a volunteer on the line during the smaller, but deadly, Blackwater fire of '37, even if he was underage. He doesn't want a repeat.*

*"Not on my watch, goddamnit," he mutters to himself.*

"You want some more coffee, Jon?"

Jonathan VanStavern looked out the dark window. You could see it was snowing again if you looked at the barn light, but it wasn't snowing hard. "If you have it," he told Joshua, pushing his cup across the table.

"How about a roll or a sandwich?"

VanStavern considered the time. Then he considered his friend. *What the hell.* "Sure, why not?"

"Kristian was a high energy person, Jon. You know that. Hell, she had to be to accomplish all that she had at her age. She had had to put herself through college by working part time, and she still graduated in four years from Berkeley's school of architecture. But I always had the feeling that she had missed a lot by growing up so fast and focusing her attention so narrowly, and that she was never quite so sure of herself as she made out.

"After we left the bar she took my arm as we walked, and she let me put my arm around her on the cable-car ride back to Union Street. She asked me in when we got to her place, and I think she probably meant for the night, but I had to be at work at seven and it was already after two, so I thought I'd better call it a night."

"Now I know you're lying," Anderson exclaimed.

Kristian shook her head. "And so there I was again, at two-fifteen in the morning, in exactly the same position I had been at the beginning of the week, wondering *just who was that thar' masked man.*"

*He tells her that he'll probably be too tired to be much fun tomorrow night after working all day and when she suggests doing something on Sunday, he says that he has promised his landlady he would help her do some gardening or landscaping or something like that. They make a date for Monday lunch.*

"Joshua was staying near Golden Gate Park, just off of Funston Avenue, in a room that he rented from a little old Japanese lady. And I'm not certain whether it was because I didn't believe him or because I did, but early Sunday afternoon I took a drive over that way, and, sure enough, there he was helping this little oriental woman move around dirt and rocks and shrubs until she would have her yard just so.

"That was the first time I ever saw Joshua with his shirt off, and all I can say, Mo, is that he was absolutely drop-dead gorgeous."

"Really?"

"Really. You should see him. On second thought, maybe you shouldn't." Maureen Andersen was a beautiful woman no matter what her preferences were. "Anyway, it was also the first time I saw Jenny, or Jenny-Dog as he used to call her, lying in the shade and moving only when it was necessary to reposition herself in order to keep her eyes on Josh. She wasn't much to look at. I think Josh said she was some type of Lab/coon-hound cross. She was black and brown with a little white on her chest; and she was kind of gangly and lumpy at the same time, with big dark eyes and floppy ears. He had picked her up somewhere in Oregon from a farmer who was going to shoot her because she kept having puppies, and Josh gave the man ten dollars for her and then spent another thirty-five to have her spayed."

"You told me about her. Is she the dog he used on this last rescue?"

"Yes, Jenny-Dog and one other. Can you believe it? She must be at least thirteen. You know, I don't know why, but in a funny way I always felt that Jenny and I were kindred spirits."

"Fair Maiden and White Wind," Andersen remarked, recalling Kristian's earlier story about the old Indian medicine woman in Arizona who seemed to know Joshua and Jenny-Dog even though she had never met them. That stopped Kristian cold. Then she continued.

"He seemed pleased when I stopped by, and he introduced me to his landlady. God, I've always loved the way he pronounces my name. Not *Krish-chin*, like onward Christian soldiers, but *Kris-ti-anne*, the way the French say it. We had a beer together, and then I told him I had to be going."

*The next day, and most days that week, they meet for lunch. Her office is in the financial district, just a short walk from his job site, and, besides being with him, she enjoys the looks that they get and the comments she receives from some of her co-workers who have seen him. He stands out from the college kids and the hippies as much as he does from the suits and ties, with his T-shirt and metal lunch bucket, because his boots and jeans are worn honestly and not as some sort of uniform or political statement. Yet he is always at ease, never self-conscious. She tries to be the same and insists on meeting him at the building site, but it's different. Her comfort there comes from being with him. And she knows it. He misses on Friday because he has to work through, and on Saturday they go to the beach.*

"Joshua picked me up in a red jeep pickup truck with a cap over the back in which he kept his dog." Kristian smiles as she thinks back to the first time she rode in Josh's truck, a truck she knows he still has. "He had bought the truck from some contractor in Oregon whom he had worked for and who was on the verge of going bankrupt. He had built the cap himself, and it was as nice as any I've ever seen, with paneling and insulation and louvre windows on the sides. By this time I had discarded, or at least sublimated, any ideas I had ever entertained about evening some imaginary score, and I was really enjoying just being with him. I was still on my guard a little because I still didn't know much about him, and what I did know seemed to be contrary to everything I had ever believed about guys since I was about fourteen. But as my old man would have said, my right hand was beginning to drop."

"What the hell does that mean?"

Kristian smiled. "It's a reference to boxers. When a fighter gets tired or overconfident, his right hand drops down, away from his face. Then he usually gets clobbered."

Andersen wanted to ask Kristian about her father. She decided against interrupting.

"I had pieced together a few bits and pieces of information about his life by then, like that he was born and raised near a small town in north-central Wisconsin to a father who was of Scandinavian descent and a mother who was French Canadian, or *Quebecoise* as he called it. He had joined the Navy right after high school and had served four years with the Seabees all over the world. The only time he had been back to the States was when his father had died in some kind of accident while Josh was overseas. When he told me the dates of his Navy hitch, I was able to figure out approximately how old he had to be, and for a moment or two I was a bit uncomfortable. But that didn't last long because Joshua always seemed to prefer talking about something I had done or something I was doing or wanted to do. That's the wonderful thing about him, Maureen. He's always interested in you, no matter who you are or what you are doing, and he has a way of making you feel that you are someone special.

"I began to realize, with some concern, that I was starting to enjoy the romance and mystery of this tall dark stranger who was too good to be true. I was concerned that the bubble would burst and that I would be on a real downer. And I was even more concerned that it wouldn't, and that would really screw things up."

*At the beach, they head for the north end where it's less crowded. The surf is high and still cold, and she tends to drift around the edge while he and his dog plunge in like they were born to it. He picks her up in his arms and carries her into the waves kicking and screaming and hugging him because of the cold and because of him, and she can feel how strong he really is. She's surprised that she doesn't resent his strength, as she would with most guys, and she's amazed at how secure she allows herself to feel with this man. It's a security she hasn't known for some ten or twelve years, since her father walked out.*

*They put Bain de Soleil on each other, and he starts to open up a little about some of the places he's been and the things he's done, and she comes to understand that he's been slowly working his way back home for the last five or six years, after mustering out of the Navy overseas.*

"After lunch, we walked along the surf, and later on he got involved in this touch football game with some jocks on the beach. Jesus, Maureen, watching him play was like watching the slow motion out-takes that you see on TV. Christ, you felt like there should have been music in the background.

"At first I flattered myself that he was trying to show off to impress me, but then it struck me that this was the way he did everything, and that I'd never known anyone who enjoyed life and people and the world around him as much as this man seemed to."

The writer sat mesmerized, wondering how such a beautiful story could really be true. Wondering what had gone wrong.

"We didn't get back to my place until about nine that evening. There was still some summer light out, but we were both pretty tired from all the sun and salt, not to mention the wine with lunch and the beer after the game. We didn't even shower the sand off. We just cuddled up and fell asleep on my bed. When we woke up, we made love."

"I swear, Jon, just between you and me and the wall, I hadn't really intended to make love to Kristian that night after we first went to the beach together."

Jonathan VanStavern didn't bat an eye. He was from a different generation, different rules, but he'd been around.

"Don't get me wrong, she could have been *The Girl from Ipanema* the way she carried herself along the edge of the surf, and I was enjoying being with her more and more as I got to know her better. She was beautiful and intelligent and she had an amazing eye and mind for detail. Kristian was extremely poised in most situations, and she looked people right in the eye, no matter who she was talking to. Most of all, when you were with Kristian, no matter how young she was or how beautiful she looked, no matter what she was wearing or what she was doing, you always knew that you were with a woman, and not just some girl. You know what I'm saying?"

VanStavern surely did.

"But as I got to know her better, I began to see that my first impression had been pretty close to the mark. She had come from a broken home, and she had grown up pretty fast in a lot of ways, and it seemed to me that somewhere along the line she had been burned, maybe more than once. Kris had some funny attitudes towards men too. Not so much in her thinking that most guys were after her ass, because that probably wasn't far from the mark either, but in her thinking that she was in some kind of strange competition with them, on their turf and with their rules, that she was bound and determined to play and to win. Well, I sure didn't want to play that game. And I sure didn't want her to think that I was only after her ass. But after we fell asleep in each other's arms that night, and then woke up together a few hours later, making love not only seemed like a natural thing to do, it seemed like the right thing to do."

"Wow...." Maureen Andersen was dazzled. Back in the sixties

she was still dating men. It had never been like that.

"The next morning I awoke to the smells of coffee brewing and bacon frying, and he had cut up all sorts of fruits and vegetables to go with the eggs and French-toast he was whipping up. He had already been out to take Jenny for a walk, and he had come back with a bag of fresh rolls and bread from a corner store. He came in to see if I was up, and, when he saw I was awake, Joshua bent over me and kissed me, and for a moment I thought that we might make love again. I wouldn't have minded either, but Joshua wasn't about to waste a beautiful day lying around in the sack, so I reluctantly got up. I think it was about 7:30.

"Jane was there, drinking coffee and flirting with Joshua. They hit it off right away, and Jane said if his eggs were as good as his coffee, I could have any two guys she knew in exchange for him. It was one of those things that you say kiddingly but that you really mean, and I knew Jane well enough to know that she meant it. But you know, I never worried about Joshua and Jane together because of the way he handled himself around her, and around me."

"Hah, I know Sloan. I would have been damn worried. She'd likely as not steal him and leave you with the dog. So then what happened?"

"After breakfast he rushed me to get dressed. He didn't even want to read the Sunday paper. He said we would have to stop by his place so that he could change, but he wouldn't tell me where we were going. He changed into clean slacks and a Ban-Lon shirt, but he still didn't tell me anything until we drove into the Mission district. And you could have knocked me over with a feather when I realized that we were going to a church!"

Andersen's mouth was wide open again. "You've got to be kidding me."

Kristian smiled and shook her head. "At first I thought it was his Midwestern upbringing coming to the surface after all. You know, some expiation of guilt felt the morning after the night before. But I should have known better by then. Joshua just liked to go to churches, and it didn't seem to matter what kind of church it was either. He told me once that you couldn't really get to know people, to understand them, until you spoke their language and knew what they believed and how they expressed that belief. He's been to all types of churches in the course of his travels, including some synagogues and some mosques and a Hindu temple and even some Buddhist monasteries, and I'm sure many others. The one we went to that day was Hispanic Catholic, and I just watched Joshua and followed his lead, even to the point of taking communion at the end of the service. Can you believe that?"

"It's hard," her friend told her, smiling.

"We spent the afternoon with Jenny at Golden Gate Park, flying kites and playing ball with kids. And it kept on like that all summer long. Except there was just one problem…"

"…and you know, Jon, the more time I spent with Kristian and the better I got to know her, the more I got to like her and to appreciate what a special person she was. Once you got past what she looked like and past her protective facade of bravado, you could see what a tender and creative person she really is, and I began to think that maybe I could help her enjoy herself, and life, a little more… And that was my first big mistake…"

*They're always on the hop, going places and doing things. Berkeley's campus and the panoramic hills and aromatic woods surrounding it; Chinatown and later the ballet; Muir Woods; Big Brother and the Holding Company with Janis Joplin for two dollars at California Hall. Pizza and beer after "A Man and A Woman" in Sausilito.*

*She brings him to parties that aren't exactly his favorite, and he always politely declines the dope but otherwise mixes easily, or at least finds someone interesting to talk to. Sometimes too interesting, Kristian thinks about some of the women.*

*She meets him at a back room bar poker game one Friday after work, where he's having fun but not playing too seriously, and one Saturday Kristian asks him to meet her at an old walk-up office in Western Addition where her company is doing some urban renewal work.*

"...because I guess, Mo, that I was still always keeping an eye out for a situation where I would come out on top, at least in my mind. I don't think he knew we were competing. Here I thought I could kill two birds with one stone. Bill Borsos, one of the senior architects at the firm, had been coming on to me all summer, and I wanted him to meet Joshua so he could see why he didn't stand a chance."

"I know Bill. Thinks he's a real womanizer. More like a real jerk."

Kristian nodded. "That was why I let Bill give me a ride that morning. But the most important thing was that I knew that once Josh got there, there wouldn't be anything for him to do except wait in the outer office and talk to the heavyset black woman who was the receptionist, and I didn't think even Joshua would find her too interesting. Of course, I was wrong."

Andersen smiled.

"There wasn't much of interest in the area where we were either, and the neighborhood was too rough for a white man to just casually poke around. But when I went over to the window in that stuffy office and looked across the street I saw one white person playing basketball on a playground full of blacks, and, standing out not only because he was white but because he was good, I knew right away who it was."

"...because you can't really help people change what they are," Joshua lamented. "Only they can do that. You just have to take them on their own terms, and I should have known that from the beginning."

*Masauwu called upon the Great Plumed Serpent to help test the Son of Light.*

*"Cast forth your magic Great Plumed Serpent. We must see if this pahana is truly the Son of Light."*

*The Great Plumed Serpent sent his magic in the form of lightning. His magic had the power to create life. And to take it.*

*The lightning continued throughout the night and into the early morning, an ominous prelude of things to come.*

# Chapter Four

*3:55 a.m.*
*August 25, 1972*

*From his office in Missoula, Montana, Arthur Marshall calls the Grangeville Air Center (GAC) in northern Idaho. They tell him that they might spare a team if he clears it with Boise. He calls Boise.*

*Hank Thurston calls Red Lodge and asks the Fire Command Center there to put together a couple of teams of hotshots and casuals, "... but people who know what the hell they're up against," just in case they are needed in the morning.*

*Richie Volas tries to pinpoint serious lightning strikes as best he can, from miles away, in an otherwise pitch black night.*

———∽∽———

"What was it that finally made you decide to pick up and leave San Francisco?" Anderson asked.

Kristian thought for a moment before deciding how to answer. "Joshua had been helping Jane and me renovate and decorate the house we were living in, and he never seemed to mind working in the evening or on weekends even though he had been working all day and all week. He's really a fine carpenter, and he can do everything from structural work to cabinet making. He was never impatient or in a hurry, and he would take the time to show me how to do things myself, without even being asked. I used to tell myself that if he hadn't been helping us and if we hadn't gone to that damn lumber yard out in Richmond, that things might have worked out differently. But, of course, I know better and did even then."

"Kris and I went out to this lumber yard over in the East Bay," Joshua explained, "and, while she was ordering the materials we needed, I was poking around like I always do if I have the time. I was in the decorative woods section when I came across this rough, gray-brown lumber that was being sold to people who wanted a rustic look inside their homes. I mentioned to the yard man that his *decorative* lumber looked just like the weathered siding off of old barns, and he told me that that was exactly what it was, and it was selling for around a buck-ten a board foot.

"Well, Jon, you know the rest. That got the ol' wheels to clicking because back home I knew where there were scores of old barns that people would pay you to tear down, and I started getting excited deep inside. I was ready to go home and I knew it was time."

"Since the beginning of August I knew something was wrong at his job, but I never knew just what it was."

"Really? How so?"

"Joshua had been working a lot of overtime, and I thought that he might just be a little tired. But it was more than that. He was like a combination crew foreman and Jack-of-all-trades because of his carpentry skills and the equipment experience he had picked up in the Seabees. He felt a lot of responsibility towards both the job and the men, and I wondered if they were paying him enough since he was non-union. But that wasn't the problem. Christ, I nearly fell through the floor when he told me how much he was making, because on an annualized basis it was nearly fifty per cent more than I

was earning. I was beginning to get worried, but he never really talked about it, not even that weekend we went camping in the Sierras
when he broke the news to me that he was getting ready to leave.

"I told you about camping with Joshua, didn't I?"

"Right. You told me about camping with him in the Tetons.
Sounds like he really knows what he's doing."

"That's putting it mildly. You know, it's funny, I had never really enjoyed camping, the few times I had gone, before I went with
Joshua, even though it was one of those things that our generation
was supposed to be *into*. It seems like I would always wind up cold
and wet and dirty and exhausted by the end of the trip. If you went
with other girls, you had to watch out for what types of freaks you
might run across out in the woods, and if you went with a guy, you
had to watch out for him because once in the woods his macho
complex would take over even though he probably wouldn't be able
to get a fire going."

"I know exactly what you mean."

"Camping with Joshua was different. He always knew where to
go and what to do. He knew how to stay warm and dry and how to
keep the bugs away. Josh always seemed to have exactly the right
equipment, even if it was improvised, and he never brought tons of
stuff we wouldn't need. He was always patient and relaxed out in the
woods, whether he was taking care of chores or trying to identify
some species of flora or fauna from a small paperback book he would
bring along. When he fished, he caught fish and, I would later find
out, when he hunted, he usually killed game. At night after dinner
he would help with the dishes even though he had cooked most of
the meal and had done most of the other chores during the day. It
was great. After dinner we would sit close to each other in front of a
campfire. Sometimes he would tell stories, and sometimes he would
just listen to me talk about my life. Or he would play that little
wooden flute he had picked up somewhere in his travels, or that old

harmonica he had carried around the world with him for ten years from Wisconsin."

"The flute the old Indian woman knew about!"

"Right. He knew tunes from all over the world, and sometimes he would stop and tell a story about where he had been and how it happened that he had learned that song, and I liked to close my eyes and smell the smoke and imagine myself being in those places with him and how wonderful it would have been. Because when I was with Joshua I didn't think about myself anymore, and that was what made him so different and so special to me."

"It sounds wonderful, Kris."

"He had just finished playing a tune on the wooden flute that I recognized as Copland's "Appalachian Spring," and I mentioned how much I liked it and other things by Copland.

"*Do you know the words?* He asked, and he surprised me because I didn't know there *were* any words."

"Are there?"

"It's taken from an old Shaker hymn called "Simple Gifts," and he recited the hymn, and then he was silent. I'll never forget it."

"That's really pretty," Andersen remarked after Kristian told her the words.

"I couldn't believe it, but I was almost in tears. That little poem just hit a responsive chord somewhere deep inside and brought up memories of dreams I had forgotten about since I was a little girl in a house where the parents had lost all warmth for each other – or maybe it was because I had an idea of what was to follow."

"*Kris, I'm going home soon*, he told me simply, and I knew just what he meant."

"*When...?*"

"*Soon.*"

"*Why...?*"

"*It's time...*"

*"Do you have to...?"*

"And he just said, *it's time.* We slept in sleeping bags inside a small pup tent with Jenny curled up outside between a large log and the smoky fire that made my eyes water.

"Damn it," Kristian's eyes began to water again. Andersen reached across the table and took her hand. "I don't know why it caught me so. All along I had known that it was going to happen sooner or later, and at first I really didn't care much. But as I got to know him, and once I finally stopped playing my silly games, it became harder and harder for me to imagine what life would be like without him. I mean, I really couldn't see myself going back to going out with some of those shmucks and ass-holes I had gone out with before, and sometimes I would remember what my life had been before I met Joshua and I would shudder." Kristian gave an involuntary shake of her head. "I guess in my fantasies I saw his job going on for a year or so, during which time Jane would move out, and Joshua would move in with me. Or I would move out, and Josh and I would find some place and live together in the Berkeley hills or maybe even in Marin. My career would take off, and I knew Josh could always find work."

"But it didn't work out that way..."

Kristian shook her head. "I knew deep down that these were just fantasies and that sooner or later Joshua would leave, and I had planned to be stoic and heroic, stiff upper lip and all that crap, because I had worked too damn hard and too damn long to get to where I was, and I wasn't going to let anything get in my way. Not anything!"

"God, Kris, what did you do?"

"That last week went by pretty fast, Jon. Too damn fast, what with packing up and getting ready to go and knowing it was my last week with Kristian. We had become more involved with each other than I think either of us had intended, and saying goodbye wasn't easy. I had planned to leave early that Saturday morning, so's I could get a good hop on the day, and we said goodbye the night before at her place, because I knew if we slept together it would be more difficult in the morning. Before I turned in, I called the building inspector and suggested that he might want to get out to the job around six-thirty or seven to take some core samples of the concrete that was being poured, instead of waiting until after eight or nine...."

"Pouring wet?" VanStavern asked. Joshua nodded.

"At around 4:30 am, I went out to the truck, ready to go, and, Jonathan, I swear I couldn't believe my eyes. There on the curb, curled up in a sleeping bag against a backpack and a suitcase by the rear wheel of the truck was Kristian!"

"No fooling?" VanStavern smiled. He could just see it. Joshua poured himself another shot of C.C.

"She had been there for over half an hour so's to make sure she wouldn't miss me. And damn, if Jenny-Dog ever even barked."

*Gogyeng Sowuhti closes her eyes and controls her breathing as she enters her vision. She must remain calm and alert if she is to help the Son of Light. She knows that this challenge will be unlike any he has faced before.*

*Forest fires usually start small and often end that way. But sometimes, if conditions are right (or wrong, depending on your point of view) they can blow up quickly and begin to run. And they can outrun any animal that lives in the forest. And any human.*

# Chapter Five

*5:00 a.m.*
*August 25, 1972*

*Richie Volas looks out towards the east and the promise of dawn. That is, he hopes it is the promise of dawn that he is seeing. He makes his scheduled call to his supervisor.*

*"I've got six possibles marked down. All to the northeast. Still can't confirm anything."*

*"Good job, son. I'll get Mitch Walker to fly over the area as soon as the sun comes up. Then we'll assess the situation and get some teams in where we need them."*

*"Anything else I should be doing?" Volas asks.*

*"You're doing fine, son. Keep doing what you're doing and call me in an hour. Should be light by then. Make sure you check in all directions. Watch the northeast especially, but don't get hung up and miss something somewhere else."*

*Volas swallowed hard. That was exactly what he had been doing, concentrating on one direction. He prayed he hadn't missed anything.*

---

"Forgive me, Kris, but I have to ask, what happened? Why did you leave? I mean, it's obvious that you were in love with this man.

Hell, you talk about him as if he's almost a god. So what happened? Country life not all it's cracked up to be?"

Kristian smiled again. "Actually it was pretty nice. For a while. That first year was so great being with Joshua. Everything was new and beautiful and interesting and exciting, and nothing seemed threatening with him close by. He would take care of chores and maintenance easily and routinely, and he got me into the rhythm of country life that was full and relaxed at the same time."

"Sounds idyllic."

"In some ways it was. Of course minor problems arose, but when they did Josh would take care of them methodically and without getting bent out of shape. He seemed to be prepared for anything, or at least able to handle anything that occurred, and I felt safer and more secure with him than I had since I was a little girl."

Andersen knew Kristian was stalling. Her experience told her to listen patiently while her friend worked her way up to whatever it was she needed to tell.

"The first thing we had to do was get the well and septic system back on line. Once that was taken care of, we were able to put the house back in shape in short order. Joshua let me take the lead in decorating, and he seemed genuinely pleased with my ideas that enhanced the light and space while maintaining the rugged, rural *Quebecois* charm of the homestead.

"I remember Josh bought an old green Oliver tractor and spent a month rebuilding it. But once he had it finished it ran like a top, and he was able to clear what he called *pioneer growth* from some land he wanted to plant in the spring. I helped with the tractor, and I helped design and build a passive solar greenhouse, attached to the house, that we used both for heat in the winter and to start many of the plants and vegetables for our garden in the spring.

"I was feeling really good about myself. I was proud that I was learning to do things with my hands that had always been traditionally male oriented tasks, especially back then. And I loved Joshua for involving me and teaching me and not being the least bit patronizing or condescending. He even taught me to shoot rifles and shotguns, and he always invited me to go hunting and fishing with him."

"Hmm…Really? Hunting and fishing?" Andersen raised an eyebrow. She had a hard time picturing it at first. But then, maybe not.

"Uh huh. I liked going fishing and bird hunting with Joshua, especially the grouse, but I knew he preferred to be alone when he went after large game, and I was just as happy to stay in bed on those cold November mornings."

"That would have been my choice."

"I was feeling proud and confident and happy that things were working out so well. We started a business tearing down old weathered barns and marketing the lumber. It was a good business because people would pay us to take down their structures, and then we would sell the lumber to builders, first locally and later throughout the country. Josh took care of locating the barns and taking them down. I was in charge of marketing. And we both took care of the books. Best of all was the fact that I could use at least some of my talent and training as an architect to draw up sketches and designs as marketing tools. Joshua always said it was my drawings that made our business the success that it was, but really we were a team. A good team."

"Sounds great. So…?"

"Everything was all so wonderful, I started worrying that the bubble might burst. We would take hikes in the woods and through the fields, and later, after we got the horses, we would go for early summer morning or autumn moonlight trail rides. We would go cross-country skiing or snow-shoeing in the winter, and when we came in we would fool around on the rug in the den in front of a roaring fire in the fieldstone fireplace."

"Gee, Kris, maybe you'd better stop. I don't want this fairytale to end." Kristian nodded, but Andersen was glad she continued.

"It all seemed so good and so right that I even started thinking about going off the pill so that I could give Joshua the children and family that I knew he wanted more than anything."

*Now we're getting somewhere.* "*He* wanted? What about you?"

"Hmm, good question. I thought I did. At least I thought I wanted to do anything that would make Joshua happy, and I knew *that* would make him happy. Looking back, of course, you always remember the good things and the happy moments. The bad things get glossed over and seem insignificant, the way you never see mosquitoes in Sierra Club calendars, and you wonder how you could have been such a fool to give up all you had. But I remember the day that things began to change. In fact, I can even pinpoint the exact moment." Kristian frowned.

Joshua and his guest sipped their drinks, savoring the warmth of the fire and the whiskey and their friendship.

"Did Kris say when she might be back?"

"No, but I'm not holdin' my breath."

Jon hesitated but then figured, what the hell, they're good friends.

"You know," he begins, "she hated it when you went out on searches. She was just plum scared to death, especially during Cody and then after."

"I know, Jon. I didn't know for a long time because I was so damn thickheaded I couldn't see what was plain before my eyes. But I surely know now."

"Did you ever tell Kris what really happened? I mean all of it?"

Joshua looked at VanStavern. "How could I?"

"Did I tell you, Mo, that I actually went out on Joshua's first rescue with him?"

Anderson perked up. "No, you didn't."

"Yeah. It was a beautiful summer evening almost ten years ago. We were asked to help look for two kids lost near the lake by the state game preserve. That was the first time Joshua ever used Jenny to find lost kids."

"What happened?"

"I nearly died, that's what happened."

"Really?"

"Well, no, not really, I suppose. But I sure as hell felt like I was going to die. I was exhausted; I couldn't catch my breath. I was drenched in sweat and scratched and bruised over most of my body."

"Did you find the kids?"

"Oh, sure. We found the kids within forty-five minutes. They were fine."

"But it was a difficult rescue?"

"Well, no, that's the thing. It was an easy rescue, at least for Joshua and Jenny-Dog. One of his easiest. That's the whole point. It gave me a frame of reference for Joshua's other rescues, some of which went on for days."

Maureen Andersen was just beginning to appreciate what Kristian must have gone through over the weekend. She regretted not staying with her longer. "So Joshua's becoming involved in rescue work affected your relationship?"

"Well, no, not at first. Oh, it got Joshua involved in one more thing, but that didn't matter, really. He still had plenty of time for me. Then, after his second rescue things began to change."

"How's that?"

"Things didn't go as smoothly as on the first rescue. He had this crazy dog that he used who didn't exactly mind like he should have. – God, there's a story I'll have to tell you sometime. The weather was colder and it was during hunting season."

"Was it another child?"

Kristian nodded.

"And was he found alive?"

"Oh sure. They found the child just fine."

"So what was the problem?"

"The problem was that Joshua realized he was involved in life or death situations. It wasn't just some game or a romp in the woods. And I don't think he ever bargained for that. All he ever really wanted was to lead a nice quiet life raising a family and doing the outdoorsy kinds of things that he loved."

"Why didn't he just stop?"

Kristian looked at her friend. "You don't know Joshua. He could walk away from football and a college scholarship and a possible pro career and never blink an eye. But he could never turn his back on a person who needed his help, especially a child."

"So he went into it whole hog," Andersen surmised.

"Whole hog and then some."

"And that affected your relationship..."

"Well, no, not really, not at first. Not until I decided to try to become pregnant, and then actually did become pregnant. Because, Mo, I would lie there at night, with him out on a rescue, and I would imagine what he was going through and all sorts of things. And I knew that that first rescue we went out on was a best-case scenario. And I would lie there, alone. And I would become scared to death for him. And I would become scared to death for me."

"Did he know how you felt?"

"I don't think so, not really. He always downplayed the danger. But he always trained harder after each rescue, no matter how well it went. And he didn't understand that the only reason I was happy living out in the wilds of Wisconsin was because I was with him. I don't know what I would have done if something had happened to him, especially if I had a baby. Does that make any sense?"

Maureen Andersen thought before she spoke. She knew that

Kristian had once been pregnant and had lost the baby during her second trimester. "Sure, it makes a lot of sense. You wanted to have some security, some control over your life. I can appreciate that. The only thing is, nothing ever happened to him."

Now Kristian hesitated. This was it. "No, that's not true. Something did happen to him."

"Really?"

"Yes. You see, as time went by, Joshua and his dogs developed quite a reputation. At first the rescues were pretty routine, local stuff like lost hunters or kids who wandered off. But after a year or two Josh started getting calls from farther and farther away. And to places more and more remote. Quite often other dog teams had been used before Joshua ever got to the scene..."

"Like last week, in Vermont."

"Exactly. Dog teams had tried and failed. That meant that not only was Josh late in getting to the scene, but it was also more difficult for the dogs to get a scent and find the trail."

"Did Joshua's success rate – What did you call it? His live find rate? – go down?"

Kristian took a sip of water. "That was the amazing thing. It really didn't. Not when the people were still alive when Josh got the call. But the rescues took their toll on him and on me, especially when they were at night or in winter or if they lasted for more than one day."

"I can imagine."

"Objectively, I knew that Joshua could take care of himself. But when I was at home all by myself, alone out in the middle of nowhere, all sorts of horrible scenarios played out in my mind, and one of them eventually came true."

"'But he always came back unhurt, didn't he?"

"He always came back. He and his teams were so good that in 1971 he got invited to lead a seminar for search-and-rescue teams that the Forest Service put on out in the Tetons. They put us up at

Colter Bay Lodge and treated us like kings."

"Nice perk."

"We thought so at the time."

"It wasn't?"

"Oh, it was a wonderful trip. Jenny-Dog thought she was in heaven."

*Once again, they are high in the Teton Mountains. Once again, they have hiked in. Once again, the air is fragrant and cool. Late summer wildflowers and grasses blossom in the high mountain meadow. Nearby is a cold, clear lake. Wildlife abounds. A fast flowing stream, just out of sight, can still be heard, background for the cry of the hawk. Joshua and Kristian make camp. Jenny-Dog chases ruffed grouse. This is the way it's supposed to be, Jenny-Dog thinks to herself.*

"Food and accommodations were great, weather just right. The problem was that Joshua made some good friends with some of the people he met out there. And I'm certain he made a strong impression on everyone who saw his dogs or participated in his demonstrations. And a lot of the people there were law enforcement personnel. One in particular was a sheriff from Cody, Wyoming."

"Out near Yellowstone, you said. What happened?"

"What happened...?" Kristian contemplated the situation. She knew that this was where her story would lead, what she had bought in for. She just wasn't certain she could go through with it. "That's a good question. We never did find out everything, at least I didn't. And I don't think Joshua did either, but he never talked about it anyway. What I did learn, I learned from Jonathan VanStavern and from reading the transcript of an inquiry held by the U.S. Forest Service about a month after the rescue."

"An inquiry?" Andersen looked surprised. "Why was there an inquiry?"

"Like I told you, there was a fire." Kristian paused and looked at her friend. It was now or never. She took a breath. "Not everyone made it out." Then she ordered a Scotch. A double.

*Gogyeng Sowhuti sits in a rocking chair on the roof of the pueblo. She is still facing north. Her eyes are now open but unblinking. Her children and grandchildren know not to disturb her.*

*"Masauwu, he is the Son of Light. He has been tested many times and each time he has been successful. Do not test him again."*

*"Only his body and his mind have been tested," Masauwu replies. "Now we must test his spirit."*

*The second strike ignited an Englemann spruce west of Native Lake on the Wyoming side of the border. Additional strikes near Burnt Bacon, Throop, and Upper Granite Lakes spread quickly, ravaging dozens of acres of summer dried timber in both the Gallatin and Shoshone national forests.*

# Chapter Six

*5:30 a.m.*
*Friday, August 25, 1972*
*Lincoln County, Wisconsin*

*The predawn sky is black and filled with stars. The air is gently cool. A nice dew lies over the fields, but the hay will be dry by ten o'clock. Joshua Travis finishes his morning chores loosely shadowed by three dogs, including Jenny who stays close. He stands tall and unencumbered, pausing to take it all in. He breathes deeply, losing himself in the aroma of freshly cut alfalfa. His soul is warmed by the light that glows in the kitchen window. The tang of bacon frying and coffee perking mixes with the wood smoke from the fire he has lit in the wood-burner to take the chill off. He knows that his wife is up. He also knows there will be eggs waiting and probably pancakes or French toast. If he is lucky, there might even be cinnamon buns baking, although he usually has to wait until Sunday for those.*

*This is the way it's supposed to be, Joshua knows. Weather is good. Farm is in order. The business has taken off. Kristian seems happy. All they need are a couple of kids around the place and everything will be just about perfect. Yep, this is the way it's supposed to be.*

---

"That summer in northern Wisconsin had been one of the nicest since I got out there," Kristian recalled. "And, from what Josh and the neighbors said, I guess it was one of the nicest in recent memory. The days were warm and dry. The nights had been cool and good for sleeping. It seemed like it rained only in late afternoon or at night or maybe on an occasional Sunday. It had been a summer that was good for working and for growing things, good for fishing in the early morning or at dusk, and good for swimming and swinging from ropes over the Wisconsin River if you were a kid, or thought you were."

"And I take it Joshua thought he was a kid."

"You should have seen us swing from that rope, holding on to each other for dear life and then plunging into the ice cold water twenty feet below."

"Tarzan and Jane."

"Exactly. But I guess the summer hadn't been so good out west. Out there it had been hot and dry since May, which was good for the tourists and the campers, but bad for the trees. And in Wyoming, about sixty-five miles northwest of Cody, not too far from Beartooth Pass, a teenage girl and her brother were out chasing a grizzly bear named Sophie with their biologist parents. From what I got from the transcript, this time the problem wasn't lack of experience, but over confidence. The family had gone in too far to get help quickly. And the lightning from the night before had started several fires, but the smoke was only visible from above the forest canopy."

"You got all this from the transcript?"

"From the transcript and from talking to people."

"How did you get a hold of the transcript?"

"Jonathan got it. He brought it over one night when Joshua was out training."

*"I doubt that Joshua wants to go over it again, Kris, but I thought you might want to see it. It might help."*

*"Thank you, Jonathan."*

*"I gotta tell you, Kris, it's not pretty."*

Kristian's lip quivered. Maureen Andersen reached across the table again and took her hand.

"Tell me, Kris. What happened?"

"They interviewed anyone and everyone who had anything to do with the fire that night, or the day before for that matter. Maybe it was just me, but from the beginning I got the feeling that they were looking for a scapegoat, somebody to pin the blame on, preferably not with the Forest Service, or at least with Forest Service policy. They were getting a lot of pressure from a well-known rancher who was gearing up for a lawsuit."

"Did they find one, a scapegoat, that is? Don't tell me they tried to blame things on your husband."

"No, not really. I suppose they just wanted to find out what happened. But there was a sharp tone to some of the questions. Like I said, maybe it was just me. They started with the testimony from the ranger who first called in the fires."

# Findings of the Joint U.S. Forest Service – Park County, Wyoming Board of Fire Review
## September 14, 1972
## Commissioner Robert J. Harrison, presiding

**Harrison:** Please state your name and position for the record.

**Volas:** Richard Volas, deputy ranger at the Crandall Ranger Station.

**Harrison:** You were on duty at the Clay Butte lookout tower the morning of August 25th of this year?

**Volas:** Yes, sir.

**Harrison:** Tell us what happened that morning, son.

**Volas:** At 6:03 a.m. I spotted several plumes of smoke to the north and northeast of Clay Butte. I immediately radioed Crandall Station and reported the fires to Mr. Thurston.

**Harrison:** That would be Mr. Henry Thurston, Supervising Ranger for the Shoshone National Forest?

**Volas:** Yes, sir.

**Carton:** What had the night before been like, Mr. Volas.

**Volas:** There had been violent thunder storms from about 11:40 p.m. to about four or four-thirty a.m.

**Carton:** Rain?

**Volas:** No, sir, at least not at the Butte. Just thunder and lightning.

**Harrison:** Did you report these conditions to your supervisor?

**Volas:** Yes, sir.

*6:04 a.m.*
*Friday, August 25, 1972*
*Clay Butte, Wyoming*

"Mr. Thurston, are you there?" Volas called over the radio. He already knew the answer.

"Up and at 'em, Richie. What you got, son?"

"I see two smokes almost due north. I make 'em to be five to seven miles out. Then there's another one north-northeast, closer in, probably around Native Lake. Oh, shit...!"

"What is it, son?"

"Two more plumes in the north, probably somewhere around Thiel Lake. I'm guessing that's the one I first called you about last night."

**Harrison:** And what were your instructions?

**Volas:** You mean that night, or in the morning?

**Harrison:** That night.

**Volas:** Hank told me to keep an eye out and to call in if I spotted anything.

**Baxter:** But you didn't call in until three-thirty a.m.?

**Volas:** Yes, sir. Didn't spot anything for sure before then.

**Harrison:** What do you mean, "for sure"?

**Volas:** There were flashes of light most of the night. I took them to be lightning.

**Carton:** Could they have been fires?

**Volas:** I don't think so, sir.

**Carton:** Why not?

**Volas:** Too sporadic and too broad. Not like the crackling bolts from about three-thirty on. And if they had been fires, wouldn't they have been continuous?

**Harrison:** How long have you worked for the Forest Service, Mr. Volas?

**Volas:** This was my first summer.

**Baxter:** Had you ever seen a forest fire before?

**Volas:** No, sir.

**Harrison:** What were your instructions when
  you reported the fires in the morning?
**Volas:** Hank, er, Mr. Thurston told me to
  close off the trailhead.


"Okay, son, now here's what we're gonna do. First off, I want you to close off the trailhead, understand? Nobody goes in except for authorized personnel. Got any people in the area now?"

"I don't think so. We had some day-trippers go in yesterday, but they're out. Don't see any new cars. Oh yeah, those friends of yours, the biologists, they might still be in. I see their Scout still parked in the corner."

"Okay. You close the trailhead. I'll call Rita over at Spirit Mountain and have them overfly the area, then I'll call it in and head up your way."

"What about your friends?"

"I don't think we have to worry too much about them. They're pretty savvy folks. I'll tell Rita to have Mitch keep an eye out for them. If we get a read on their position, maybe we can get a message to them, pluck them out if necessary."

"Yes, sir. Anything else?"

"Just sit tight and keep a lookout. I may need you to pull a double shift. Is that okay?"

"Yes, sir. No problem."

"Good man. Let's get cracking."


**Harrison:** To your knowledge, was there any-
  body in the area of the fires?
**Volas:** There was no way of knowing for sure.
**Carton:** Had anybody used the trailhead that
  had not returned?
**Volas:** Yes, sir. The Barstow family.

**Harrison**: And you reported this to Ranger
   Thurston.
**Volas**: Yes, sir. I knew he would want to
   know. I mean, they were friends of his.
**Harrison**: Any other questions for this
   witness?
**Baxter**: What was the wind like that morning?
**Volas**: At six a.m. the winds were light, out
   of the southwest.
**Carton**: Define "light".
**Volas**: Five to ten miles per hour or less.
**Harrison**: Anything else? Thank you, Mr.
   Volas. You may take your seat.

At 9,811 feet, Clay Butte was the highest accessible point in the immediate vicinity. The lookout tower did not have to be perched high off the ground to provide unobstructed views of the surrounding area. The three-story tower was more akin to a three-season porch set atop a tapering two-story base. The base had an additional stone porch-like addendum, added during the recent renovation. It had originally been built in 1942 but was decommissioned in the late sixties when the powers-that-be decided that airplanes were more efficient. It was being renovated for use as an information station and tourist attraction.

But Hank Thurston had never fully bought into that way of thinking, and he still used the tower for training his new rangers and his summer temps. There was ample room for men and radio equipment, two cots and a wood stove. At 9,811 feet you needed the stove, even in August, but the view of gently sloping meadows and surrounding mountains and valleys was spectacular. And the base was large enough to store plenty of equipment.

Volas climbed down the tower's ziggurat style staircase. He

walked across the gravel parking lot to the iron guard rail gate, swung it closed and locked it with a chain and padlock. He looked out to the north. The smoke from two of the plumes was connecting at the top and spreading out. The scent of wood smoke filled his mind. At that moment, Richie Volas was not sure whether or not this was why he had signed on.

*Damn.*

*"Yaponcha", Masauwu called to the wind god, "come use your magic and help us test the Son of Light."*

*Over one hundred acres were in flames before the fires were first detected and confirmed at sunrise. At seven am the winds began kicking up.*

# Chapter Seven

"You know, Josh, that I shared the transcript from that damn Joint Review Board with Kristian."

"I know, Jonathan. Kristian told me."

"She read it from beginning to end. Asked me all sorts of questions. A lot of them I didn't have an answer to. Still don't. I guess I thought maybe it would help. Probably should have kept my nose out of it. You ever read that transcript, Josh?"

Joshua sat in silence and sipped his drink. "No."

"So your husband never read the transcript?"

Kristian shook her head.

"For God's sake, why not?"

"It was a real nightmare. He had lived through it once. Then they dragged him through it a second time at the inquiry. Why on earth would he want to relive it again?"

"It was that bad?"

Kristian paused a moment.

"Worse. The next person to testify was the ranger in charge at the time."

**Harrison:** Mr. Thurston, you are the supervising ranger for the Shoshone National Forest?

**Thurston:** Northern half.

**Harrison:** I beg your pardon?

**Thurston:** Supervising ranger for the northern half of the Shoshone National Forest.

**Harrison:** Yes, thank you. Now, Mr. Thurston, you have heard Mr. Volas' testimony. Is there anything you would like to add or correct?

**Thurston:** No, sir.

**Harrison:** Mr. Thurston, was it unusual to have an inexperienced man manning an observation post during fire season?

**Thurston:** Most of our summer people are inexperienced, at least at the beginning of the summer. They're pretty well seasoned by the end of August. Richie did his job.

**Carton:** Mr. Thurston, why didn't you tell Mr. Volas to report anything suspicious as soon as he saw it?

**Thurston:** I did and he did.

**Carton:** Excuse me, sir, but he did not. Mr. Volas testified that he saw flashes during the night.

**Thurston:** During a thunderstorm.

**Carton:** Wouldn't you be interested in suspicious flashes during a thunderstorm?

**Thurston:** I'm always interested in what takes place during a thunderstorm during fire season.

**Baxter:** Then why didn't you instruct Mr. Volas to inform you about anything suspicious during the night of August 24th and the early morning of the 25th.

**Thurston:** I did and he did. All of our spotters have standing orders to report any
fires or anything they suspect might be a
fire. It is neither practical nor possible
for them to report every flash of lightning that takes place during the summer.

**Harrison:** But we now know that at least some
of the flashes Mr. Volas saw before 3:30
that night were probably fires.

**Thurston:** I don't know that we do, but hind-
sight is always twenty-twenty. And there's
not much I could have done that night anyway. I wasn't about to send a plane or
a chopper into a thunderstorm at night
in the mountains. I called Supervisor
Marshall in Missoula and told him we might
need some teams in the morning. We as-
sessed the situation as soon as we could
and acted on that information.

Hank Thurston phoned the Cody airfield. One of his old high school sweethearts answered the call.

"Spirit Mountain Aviation..."

"Morning, Rita. Has Mitch taken off yet?"

"Hank? Why no, honey. His first charter is an eight o'clock. You'll have to wait 'til then to see me."

"Doubt it'll be today, sweetheart. Is Mitch handy?"

"He's right here, Hank. Trouble?"

"Hope not. Can I talk to him please?"

"Sure thing." She handed the phone to her husband. A serious look crossed her eyes.

"What's up, Hank?"

"We got some plumes north of Clay Butte. One looks to be pretty fair size. Any chance you could fly over the area, let us know exactly what we're dealing with? What direction they're moving and the like?"

"Sure thing, partner. I can be airborne in fifteen. Should be back in an hour or so. Plenty of time for my eight o'clock."

"Uh, one other thing, Mitch. Keep a lookout for any hikers and such, will you? I know there's at least one family somewhere in the area, maybe around Granite Lake. Think you can buzz around a little, try and get a fix on their location?"

"What the hell's a family doing up there? Bear country, ain't it."

"You got it. That's why they're there. Couple of biologists and their kids tagging a she-bear and her cubs. Friends of mine, actually. I'm sure they're okay. They all know their way around the woods pretty good. I'd just like to know where they are for sure. Just in case we have to pluck them out."

"Will do, Hank. Want me to send Rick up in the chopper?"

"I'd be obliged. Ah, I probably ought to tell you, wind's pickin' up a little up here."

"Yeah, here too. But we'll get him up before the sun stirs things up too much. Want us to take them out if we spot them?"

"Probably not a bad idea. At least have Rick talk to them. Let them know what's what."

"You got it, Hank. What's your radio frequency?"

"118.6"

"Got it. We'll get right to it."

"Thanks, buddy. I owe you one."

"Speaking of which, where you want me to send the bill?"

"Cody office."

The Cody office of the United States Forest Service, located one mile west of town on Sheridan Boulevard, did not open to the public until 8:00 a.m. Until then it was manned by another one of the summer rangers, usually a college student like Volas. Thurston called the office and officially reported the fires at 6:13. He told the ranger to call District Headquarters in Missoula immediately and to inform Fire Supervisor Arthur Marshal. Thurston would call Missoula himself as soon as he got the assessment from Mitch Walker in the air.

Next, Thurston called the people under his command, whether they were scheduled to be on duty or not. He wanted all hands available in case they were needed. For the moment, most of the fires looked to be in free burn zones covered by the new policy. But you never knew. This summer had been the driest year since 1910, and the forest was a powder keg. The wind was beginning to kick up, and, while at the moment the blazes appeared to be deep inside the wilderness area, it wouldn't take much to send the fires towards Cooke City or even Silver Gate. Just to be on the safe side, Thurston called Red Lodge and asked to have two teams of firefighters rounded up. He also decided to call Missoula, Montana himself and make certain a team of jumpers and a couple of DC-6 fire suppression planes were on the way. Then he called the guest ranch.

**Carton:** Mr. Thurston, why did you delay calling the district office?

**Thurston:** I didn't.

**Carton:** Excuse me, sir, but you just testified that you called the airport first, and then you called the Cody office. Why didn't you call the District One office as soon as you got reports of the fires?

**Thurston:** I knew Mitch usually had early morning charters. I wanted to be sure I caught him before he took off. I called the Cody office to make sure they knew about the situation. They called Region One Headquarters. Then I called Missoula also.

**Harrison:** Can you tell us approximately how much time elapsed between the time you first learned about the fires and the time you called them in to the District One office?

**Thurston:** I called the fires in to the Cody office at 6:13. You can check with Supervisor Marshall, but I think you will find that he learned about the fires two minutes later.

**Carton:** But you didn't talk to Mr. Marshall until approximately 6:30.

**Thurston:** After dawn? That sounds about right.

**Baxter:** And why was that?

**Thurston:** There wasn't much I could add at the time. I wanted to make sure I caught all of my people, and I wanted to line up the fire crews from Red Lodge.

**Harrison:** Wouldn't it have made more sense to line up the smokejumpers first?

**Thurston:** The smokejumpers were lined up. Arthur was already on it. The first team landed around 7:30, as soon as we knew where to put them. I knew that the winds would be picking up, and I didn't know about the availability or feasibility of jump teams later in the day. I figured it

would take time to round up the Red Lodge
crews and get them on site. I wanted to
make sure we had at least one more crew
on the way in case more jumpers weren't
available or couldn't get in.

**Carton:** It seems like those are good reasons
for calling the smokejumpers first.

**Thurston:** Maybe, but Supervisor Marshall
had already been alerted since 4:00 a.m.
I knew he would start moving on the jump
teams, if any were available.

**Carton:** I see. What did you do next?

**Thurston:** I called the guest ranch at Hunter
Peak.

"Hunter Peak..."

"Good morning, Sandy..."

"Hank? Didn't expect to be hearin' from you this time of the morning."

"Sorry to be calling during breakfast. I know you're busy."

"Never too busy for you, Hank. Whatchya need?"

"I was just wondering when you expected the Barstows back?"

"Expectin' 'em any time, but I guess that all depends a lot on Sophie."

Sophie was the bear they were tracking.

"They're booked right through the weekend, but they usually like to spend a day or two unwinding before heading back. Want me to give you a call when they show up."

"Yeah, I'd appreciate that. But listen, I might be a little hard to get a hold of, so don't call Crandall. Just call Cody and leave a message. I'll keep checking."

"Anything wrong, Hank."

"Well, to tell you the truth, Sandy, we got a few fires spotted north of Clay Butte."

"That's the area they were heading, isn't it?"

"Afraid so."

"Want me to send Jill and Charlie over with a couple of horses? They can trailer 'em to the trail head and then ride in."

"Ah, I don't know yet, Sandy, but thanks for the offer. We got the trailhead closed, and we don't know for sure where the Barstows are. I'd just as soon keep people out of the area if I can, especially on horseback. I got Mitch Walker taking a look. If we need help notifying people in the area I may call."

"Well don't you hesitate, Hank. Our horses are rock steady and so is Jill, so you just call if you need us. You hear?"

"I'll surely do that, Sandy. Right now, I'm hoping it won't come to that."

"Well, you just call if there's anything you need."

"I will. Thanks."

There wasn't much else Hank Thurston could do for the moment, not until he heard back from Mitch Walker. Thurston had dealt with wildfire before. He knew that fire was a part of the forest ecosystem, as were rain and wind and soil. All the same, this time he was worried. Maybe it was the relatively new let burn policy for wilderness areas, easy to decide in an office or college classroom, much harder to implement when faced with decisions on the ground. Maybe it was that he had friends near the fire zones, even if they were wilderness savvy. Wildfires were tricky and unpredictable, especially in a year that had been bone dry, he reminded himself. Supervising Ranger Hank Thurston decided it was time to drive up to the lookout at Clay Butte.

*Massauwu was the Spirit of Death and the Keeper of Fire. The people were charged to watch for the Pahana, but it was Massauwu who would put Him to the test.*

*Gogyeng Sowuhti asked the Shoshone People to send someone to help the Son of Light.*

*The hot, dry summer had cured the forests to kindling and tinder. Relative humidity dropped below ten percent. Ninety years of mistaken policy, just recently changed, had put out all fires as soon as possible and left the area well supplied with dead wood. A decades long infestation of mountain pine beetle killed many trees, leaving giant matchsticks swaying in the wind. Pine needles and pitch cones on the forest floor contained as little as two percent moisture. The deadfall was drier than kiln dried lumber. Trees began to explode deep within the burn, sending their showers of flaming embers skyward; fiery scouts seeking new fronts against which to advance.*

# Chapter Eight

*Jonathan VanStavern got up and walked to the wood-burner. He picked up the enameled steel coffee pot and refilled his cup.*

*"You know, Josh, I've read that transcript many times."*

*Joshua looked at his friend. "I figured you had."*

*"I also talked to Mick Dugan about it a lot."*

*Joshua knew this also. He just looked at his friend.*

*"Thurston did everything right. You all did."*

*"Yeah? Tell that to Guy Macauley."*

<center>~~~</center>

No one needs to remind Guy Macauley that 1972 has been bone dry. At six-thirty in the morning he is already running a half-hour late.

"Let me off at the house, then leave the truck over by the hay barn, son. Then c'mon in for breakfast. I got to call in. You did a good job, son, and I thank you," Macauley let his ten-year-old boy know.

Billy nodded stoically, trying not to beam. Inside he was bursting with pride. Bringing hay out to the cattle had become a morning ritual all month. He and his father would get up at 4:30 and generally finish by six or six-thirty, depending on where the animals happened to be. He would drive the old Dodge Power Wagon that his dad had converted into a stake truck, while his father tossed off bales of hay to the drought hungry animals. This time his dad had let him drive the Power Wagon all the way back to the house, not an easy trick for a boy who had to slide off the seat every time he had to clutch. Now he was being trusted to drive it alone, without his dad even in sight.

Macauley entered the house through the mud room.

"Daddy!" Five year old Annie jumped into his arms.

"Morning, Pumpkin." Guy kissed his daughter. "Mmmm. You taste sweet. What's that on your face?" His daughter was covered with white powder and pale yellow goo.

"Pancakes!" his daughter explained.

"And what's this on your hands?" Macauley asked about the goo that was now on his denim shirt."

"Pancakes!"

Guy Macauley hugged his little girl. He didn't care a whit about the flour and batter that was now all over him. This was what it was all about and he knew it.

"You been helpin' momma?"

Annie nodded emphatically.

"Good girl." He hugged his daughter again and then carried her into the kitchen to search out his wife. They found her by the sink, running water into the batter bowl.

"Mornin', momma." Macauley reached around his wife's waist with his left arm, still holding Annie securely in his right, and kissed her on the cheek. "You get a hold of Mick?"

Jan Macauley smiled and backed tight into her husband. She nodded. "He said no problem, but to call him when you got in."

Macauley gave his wife a squeeze, kissed her on the neck just below her right ear, gave his daughter a peck on the nose before lowering her to a kitchen chair, and went over to the phone. He dialed the Park County Sheriff's Office located on Tenth Street in Cody.

"Morning, Mick. Sorry I'm runnin' a little late this morning. Damn cattle drifted all the way down to the bow."

Annie's face exploded with shock and glee. "Momma, daddy said a cuss word!"

Jan smiled. "Guy?"

"Sorry, guys. Those darn cattle drifted all the way to the bow. How's that?"

Sheriff Mick Dugan was patient. He was used to having these kinds of interrupted conversations with Macauley when he called in from home.

"What have you got for me, Mick?"

"Nothing pressing. Take a ride up to Clark and have a talk with Harmon and Alice again. I got a report they were up half the night screaming at each other and breaking things."

"Again?" Macauley shook his head, but he couldn't repress a small smile.

"Better get the keys. Bring 'em on in if you think it will help, and I'll have a little talk with them."

"Right. Anything else?"

"Not at the moment. Swing on down through Powell and Ralston, but give me a call from Clark. Let me know if I need to stick around. I gotta be in court this afternoon, but I'm figuring on running down to Meeteetse this morning."

"Will do. Catch you later."

Billy Macauley came in through the mud room.

"Did you wash your hands, William?" his mother asked.

"Yes'm."

Jan Macauley nodded approval as she transferred the last stack of pancakes from the griddle to the round oak kitchen table already laden with bacon and syrup, milk and cereal, butter, jam, fruit and the omnipresent peanut butter. A pot of coffee simmered on the stove. When the four people were seated, they joined hands, bowed their heads, and said their *Thankfuls*. When Macauley looked up he caught a glint in Jan's eye that he hadn't noticed before. He had a suspicion what it might be, but he wouldn't push her. She would tell him in her own good time. *Yep*, he thought, *this is what it's all about.*

*Masauwu called upon Taiowa, the sun god, to help Yaponcha and give him strength.*

*A dying old whitebark along the Burnt Bacon perimeter burned slowly at first, ignited by a glowing ember that landed at its base. The fire worked its way patiently to the crown where dead needles, branches, and cones exploded into the sky.*

# Chapter Nine

The rain picked up in San Francisco. It was a raw winter night, and Kristian was in no hurry to go home to her empty townhouse. She had blown off most of Sunday, a much needed rest from the tense, exhaustive weekend she had experienced, but she had still painstakingly prepared for the Monday morning meeting with her clients, and that meeting had gone exceedingly well. As her friend Jane had put it so delicately, what the hell was the point in being a partner if you couldn't screw off once in a while?

Jane was still in Mexico. In some ways that was probably a good thing. Jane already knew the story, and Kristian knew Jane's opinion. Jane had a way of crystallizing everything, of making everything seem so easy, so black and white. Kristian did not want that. She wanted a fresh perspective, an objective one if possible. Who better than Maureen Andersen?

Andersen finished her dessert.

"This cheesecake is downright evil."

Kristian smiled. "Want some more?"

"Hell yes I want some more, but only if you'll split it with me?"

Kristian wasn't hungry, but she agreed. Then Andersen asked her, "Who was Mick Dugan?"

Kristian took a breath. "He was the Sheriff of Park County, Wyoming. He's the one Joshua had met in the Tetons and who asked Josh to help with the rescue."

*John Patrick Michael "Mick" Dugan, High Sheriff of Park County, Wyoming, smiles as he hangs up the phone.* Guy Macauley was a good man. Rock steady, mature for his age, head on straight, unlike some vets Dugan knew. Macauley loved the county he had grown up in, and he liked most of the people. He was the grandson of a well-respected, if not overly prosperous rancher and was struggling to make it on his own. Macauley's living on a small spread in the Sunlight Basin was a plus to Dugan's way of thinking. *Kinda gives the department a standing presence in the northern half of the county.* Macauley didn't mind patrolling the mountain switchbacks, summer or winter, and he knew all of the roads, dirt or paved, and most of the trails. If Guy had to call in late now and again to keep his show running, why hell, it was a small price to pay. And Macauley was always good for the time.

Dugan knew the ranchers in the area were having a tough go this summer. Some of them would fold, and that would mean more work for his office. Dugan ran a few horses and kept a string of dogs, but he was glad his livelihood wasn't dependent on the land and Mother Nature, especially this year. The drought was one of the things that helped him decide to run for re-election come November. That and the fact that he thoroughly enjoyed his job and, if the crime statistics and local papers could be believed, he was damn good at it. "Yeah," he'd once told his wife, "sure beats workin' for a living." She knew better. They both did.

"I'm heading out for Meeteetse and Pitchfork," Dugan informed his dispatcher. "Should be back by noon. Have Terry cover Wapiti and East Gate."

"Will do, Sheriff. I got Hank Thurston on line two. Want it in your office?"

Dugan shook his head and reached over the counter to the desk phone. "Morning, Hank. We still on for lunch?"

"Afraid not, Mick. That's why I'm calling. I'm up here at Clay Butte. Just wanted to let you know we got some fires over the line. Maybe one by Native Lake too."

"Need me to do anything?"

"Not at this time, Mick. Just wanted to give you a heads up. Spread the word, we're closing the area."

"Will do, Hank. Give me a call if there's anything else you need me to do."

Thurston thought a moment, then asked, "What's the status of your chopper, in case I need that?"

"In the hanger right now for routine maintenance. Jack says she'll be up by noon. If you need something before that you'd best call Rick Littlejohn at Spirit Mountain."

Thurston winced. "Rita's looking for him now. Thought maybe you had him in the tank."

"Sorry, Hank."

"Okay, thanks, Mick."


**Harrison:** What did you do next, Mr. Thurston?

**Thurston:** As soon as I got a report from our spotter, I called Missoula to send in the first jump team. I also called Red Lodge again to make sure their teams were on the way. Then I called up my people and had them close down the trailheads and begin clearing the area of civilians.


"Clay Butte, this is Cessna SM173. Anybody down there?"

"Good morning again, Mitch. What you got?"

"Hank, I'm at 12,000 feet. You got one patch of fire north of

Granite Lake, between Thiel and Burnt Bacon lakes. I make it to be about a quarter by a quarter, maybe forty acres. Now I'm approaching another northwest of Granite. This one's a little bigger, probably sixty acres."

"Got it Mitch. What else?"

"Let me take it up a notch." Walker climbed to 15,000 feet, four thousand feet above the jagged peaks. "We got a narrow ridge of fire just southwest of Burnt Bacon, along the slope. Dependin' on wind, could link up the other two. Hard to say for sure. The wind is getting a little tricky up here."

"Anything else?"

Walker banked his plane in a gradual arc to the west. He held his turn until he had come full circle, scanning the wooded slopes below ten thousand feet.

"Don't see anything."

"What about the Native Lake area?"

"Didn't notice anything on the way up. I'll take another look on the way back."

Walker brought his small plane down to 10,000 feet, already several thousand feet lower than he was allowed to fly on a charter since some of the peaks in the area topped that altitude. He headed southeast, towards home.

"Yep, you're right, Hank. Got a small burner west of Native Lake, maybe eight or ten acres."

"Seen any sign of the Barstows or anybody else."

"Negative. Let me make another pass." This time Walker came down just above tree top. Normally he would have relished the opportunity for barnstorming, but the erratic wind made low level flying through the rugged terrain hairier than he had bargained for. He was relieved when he completed his passes and could bring the plane back up to a safe altitude.

"Don't see hide nor hair of anyone, Hank. Not even their camp.

You say they're up by Granite Lake?"

"Just a guess, Mitch. Could be anywhere."

"Well, I don't see anyone down below, Hank. Anything else?"

"Not at the moment, Mitch. Appreciate it. What about Rick?"

"Rita's tryin' to track him down. Seems he was out hound doggin' it most of the night."

"Hope she finds him. I want the area clear of tourists, especially now."

"Don't worry, partner. You know Rita. I'm gonna run my charter up to Bozeman. I'll keep my eyes open, and I'll overfly the area again on the way back."

"Much obliged, Mitch."

"Good luck."


Thurston switched channels and called back to Cody.

"Helen, patch me through to Missoula, will you."

"District One..."

"Arthur? Hank here. I'm up at Clay Butte. Just got a reading from my spotter. We got at least four fires in or near our section, probably close to a hundred acres total already. I'd like to get some teams in, pronto. Make sure things don't head south."

"Like I told you last night, Hank, you've caught me at a bad time. Only got one team of jumpers in camp, and they've only had two days' rest. My other teams are all still out. I've managed to line up a team from Boise, but it will take them a couple of hours to get there. Those fires in the burn zone?"

"We got one this side of the line, around Native Lake. The others are in the zone. I want to make damn sure they stay there. I got a couple of teams from Red Lodge forming up."

"Okay, Hank. I'll send my team in ASAP. I'll call Boise and Prescott and see what else we can line up. Where do you want my team?"

"Your call, Arthur, but I'd guess we'd best start with Native Lake. When the Red Lodge teams get here, I'll send them up to reinforce your men. Then, we can send any other teams you come up with farther north, if necessary, or wherever we might need them."

"Sounds good. On our way."

"Thanks, Arthur."

"Don't thank me 'til you see what I come up with. Over."

Next, Thurston called the Crandall Ranger Station.

"Good morning, Crandall. Laura, you there?"

"Morning, Hank. How do things look?"

"Looks like we might have the makings of a real cookout. The rest of the crew there?"

"Everyone except Jeff. He called to let us know he was running a little late. Had a flat."

"Okay, here's what I want you to do. I want all trails closed from Crazy Creek to Island Lake. Gates locked and signs posted. Should be some fire signs in the big shed."

"What about Pilot Creek and Sawtooth Lake?"

"Not at this time. We'll re-evaluate later. I want everyone with binoculars and handhelds and make sure the handhelds all have fresh batteries, and keep the truck radios on."

"This channel?"

"Yes. Team people up, at least two to a trailhead, and make sure at least one of each team is comfortable on horseback. I'm gonna call Sandy Curtis at Hunter Peak and see if we can't line up some horses to help clear the trails. I want the whole area closed and cleared."

"We're looking at seven trailheads. We only have twelve people. Want me to call in some of the others."

"Yeah, I think you'd better. Until then send just one person to Crazy Creek and one to Lake Overlook. That should be okay for now as long as they close the trails."

"Got it. Anything else?"

"That should do it for now. Let's get to it. Try to keep people from getting in. Let me know if there are any problems, and have everyone check in when they get in position."

"Talk to you in a bit. Over."

"Over."

Hank Thurston had to let the phone at Hunter Peak ring a dozen times before Sandy Curtis finally picked up.

"Sorry, Hank. We're cooking breakfast outside this morning and I didn't want the fried bread to burn."

"No problem, Sandy. Wish I could be there." Thurston had been to some of Hunter Peak's outdoor breakfast cookouts along the Clarks Fork of the Yellowstone River. The thought of scrambled eggs and venison sausage over fried bread, all cooked over a wood fire, made his mouth water and reminded him that he hadn't had anything to eat since his five o'clock cup of black coffee.

"Listen, hon, I'm gonna ask you something, and I want you to be straight with me if it's a problem. Okay?"

"Go ahead, Hank."

"I'd like to take you up on your earlier offer. I don't know if you have any trail rides scheduled today, but if you don't, you think you could get Jill and some of your wranglers to get together a string of horses to help clear some of our trails? We got some pretty good fires going and I want to make sure nobody's in the way, what with the Let Burn policy we got now." Thurston knew that the Hunter Peak horses were calm, easy to control, and sure footed in difficult terrain.

Sandy Curtis was no fan of the new policies. Trouble with Let Burn was that the dang fires didn't play fair. They didn't know or care where they were supposed to burn and where they weren't. Once a wildfire got to running, it was pretty darn hard to stop if God and the weather weren't on your side.

"I don't think we have anyone signed up for this morning, Hank.

I'll get Jill and Charlie right on it. How many horses do you want?"

"Twelve or fourteen, if you can manage it, Sandy. I'm looking to pair up one of your people with one of mine at each trailhead north of 212 between Crazy Creek and Island Lake."

"The horses won't be a problem. I'll have to call Will Shorter at Clarks Fork and see if he can loan us an extra trailer and a few hands."

"I sure appreciate this, Sandy. Bill me whatever you need to."

"Don't worry about it, Hank. Come across the Barstows yet?"

"...Not yet."

"We'll get right on it."

*Many years ago Gogyeng Sowuhti tried to control Yaponcha, the wind god. Now Massauwu called upon Yaponcha to help with the trial. Yaponcha was loose. And he was angry.*

*One hundred and fifty acres were burning at eight a.m., small by that summer's standards, healthy by the standards of forest ecology and theoretically still manageable according to the standards of the U.S. Forest Service. Then the winds changed.*

# Chapter Ten

**Harrison:** You used civilians to clear the area?

**Thurston:** Yes, sir, volunteers paired up with Forest Service people.

**Harrison:** Didn't that put you in contravention of Forest Service regulations forbidding the use of untrained volunteers?

**Thurston:** I didn't see it that way. The volunteers we used were all experienced wranglers who were familiar with the trails and the terrain. These people could have trained any trainers the Forest Service might have come up with.

**Carton:** Mr. Thurston, I'm confused. You lined up your people and the horses from Hunter Peak before you called in the smokejumpers from Region One.

**Thurston:** No, sir. The smokejumpers had already been called in and were on their way.

**Carton:** But you didn't actually call them in

until later. Is that correct?

**Thurston**: No, sir. I just didn't talk to the actual strike leader until a little later.

**Carton**: And why was that?

**Thurston**: My first priority was to close and secure the area. The largest fires were in a Burn zone and they were moving to the northeast, a good direction as far as life and property went. The Red Lodge fire teams were on the way, and I planned to use them to reinforce the jump team at the closest fire, the one west of Native Lake.

**Harrison**: How did you plan on using the smokejumpers?

**Thurston**: I planned on having them cut off the fire at Native Lake. Then I planned on leapfrogging them up north to cut fire-breaks south of the border. I wanted to keep the larger fires out of the Shoshone in case the wind changed directions.

**Harrison**: Which it did.

**Thurston**: Yes, sir, it did.

VanStavern's hackles were up.

"That damn Board of Review was out to crucify someone, any-one, so long as it got the Forest Service and their new Let Burn policy off the hook. They were under a lot of pressure from ranch-ers, including Macauley's grandfather, and from the bureaucrats and policy makers in Washington. They tried to get Thurston, even though he was one of their own. Then they tried to get Mick, and they tried to get you."

"You can't blame Guy's grandfather, Jon. Dugan told me that Guy's grandfather was half Indian, Shoshone I think, and he must have had it pretty rough back in the old days. He had lost his son in Korea and Guy was the world to him. And now this happens. And the only problem with the Let Burn policy was that it wasn't started about a hundred years ago. Those were all good people out there, especially Guy. If there was anyone to blame, I reckon it was me."

"Bullshit."

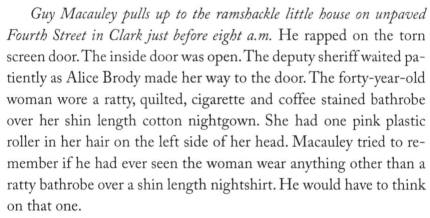

*Guy Macauley pulls up to the ramshackle little house on unpaved Fourth Street in Clark just before eight a.m.* He rapped on the torn screen door. The inside door was open. The deputy sheriff waited patiently as Alice Brody made her way to the door. The forty-year-old woman wore a ratty, quilted, cigarette and coffee stained bathrobe over her shin length cotton nightgown. She had one pink plastic roller in her hair on the left side of her head. Macauley tried to remember if he had ever seen the woman wear anything other than a ratty bathrobe over a shin length nightshirt. He would have to think on that one.

"Morning, Sheriff. What brings you out this way? – Harmon! It's Guy Macauley!"

"Tell him I'll have to catch him next time around. I'm running late," Harmon Brody called back.

"Good morning Alice. I just thought as long as I was up this way I'd get me a cup of that wonderful coffee you make." Alice Brody made the worst coffee in the state. Anybody who had ever sampled any of it and lived to tell about it referred to it as mud – when they were being polite. It wasn't all that far from the truth. "But as long as I'm here, I would like to have a word with you and Harmon."

"Says he wants to talk to me an' you, Harmon. See, I told you them neighbors would call the law on you! C'mon in Sheriff. Plenty o' coffee on the stove."

Harmon Brody made his way through the cluttered little house to the cluttered little kitchen, still drying his face with a week old towel. His graying T-shirt had a hole in it and barely covered the folds of fat that were rapidly taking over his once muscled torso.

"Now you done it, woman. I told you not to git me riled."

"Me? You was the one that broke my clock an' that mirror! – He broke my mamma's cuckoo clock, Guy, an' our mirror too."

"Well damn if she didn't have it coming, Sheriff, drinkin' the last Coors whilst I'm slavin' at work."

"Slavin' my ass. You're just washin' a few cars down at the Ford dealership in Powell. An' I told you, I didn't drink the last bottle. It was money enough for beer or beef."

Macauley poured himself a cup of coffee from the blue speck-led enamel coffeepot on the wood burning stove. He hoped it was hot enough to kill whatever germs happened to be calling the cup home that day. Then he cleared himself a spot at the messy table and shooed a cat from a vinyl chair so he could have a seat. He listened to the ragged couple going back and forth for a few minutes, exchanging accusations and blame. What else did they have in their lives to account for all they didn't have? They wouldn't blame God, and they couldn't blame themselves, so what else did they have? There was the government, of course, which, in fact, was all that stood between them and total destitution. But to criticize the government now would have put them on the side of those pinkos from the cities who were always callin' for an end to the war abroad and a redistribution of wealth in this country. Harmon supported the war in Vietnam, but he did wish the VA would up its benefits to vets who fought in a *real* war over in Korea.

Guy Macauley hoped he didn't grimace too much as he sipped

his coffee. He let the shouting and recriminations continue for another minute or two. Then he simply unbuttoned his left shirt pocket and dug out two small silver keys which he let drop onto the kitchen table. There was instant silence.

"Now hold on there, Guy, we had us a deal."

"Yes we did, Harmon, and it appears to me you've broken it."

"Now that ain't fair, Deputy. Hell, I didn't even go for the first key. Hell, I didn't even hit 'er. Tell him."

"You would of hit me with my mamma's clock if'n I hadn't ducked," Alice told him, sensing victory was hers this round.

"Hell, I knowed you was gonna duck."

"You're just lucky you didn't kill me, you old fool. Look what you done to the mirror..."

Macauley had had just about enough. Even at eight o'clock in the morning, the temperature in the stuffy kitchen was over eighty. Only the wind blowing through the broken screen window made it just barely tolerable, and it was bringing in the flies.

"Mick wants me to bring you two in. Maybe have you go up before Judge Rosenthal again."

"Now there ain't no call to do that, Deputy." Harmon Brody was becoming anxious and conciliatory at the same time. "Big Ed'll fire my ass if I miss any more days."

Guy Macauley looked Harmon Brody square in the eyes. Then he looked at Alice. He honestly felt sorry for these people. He wished there was more he could do. Then he looked at Harmon again.

"Give me the other set, Harmon."

"Do I gotta?" Brody sounded just like a little kid. Macauley almost smiled. "They're all in there, Guy. You can check for yourself."

Macauley thought for a moment. "I know they are, Harmon. But I want the keys just the same."

Harmon Brody left the room, followed by Alice.

Judge Allen Rosenthal had been at a loss as to what to do about these two. They appeared before his bench far too regularly. He knew they didn't have much. Hell, besides each other they didn't have anything. He doubted locking up one or the other or both would do much good. And neither of them had ever actually hurt the other, at least not intentionally.

But Rosenthal wanted to make a statement that would get through to them. He also wanted to send a message to the rest of the county, so he ordered Harmon Brody to lock up all his guns in a Liberty gun safe and to lock all his ammo and the key to the Liberty combination dial in a Homak safe. Then Rosenthal ordered Park County to loan Harmon and Alice Brody the eight hundred and fifty dollars that the two safes cost and to collect fifteen dollars a month until they were paid for. Harmon Brody got the combination to the Liberty. Alice Brody got to hide the key to the Homak. The Sheriff's Office kept the duplicates.

"Here you go, Deputy." He dropped the flat key on the table. Alice did the same with the ring key. "How long?"

Macauley gathered up the keys and rose.

"Depends on you two. Just remember folks, huntin' season's not far off. If I have to come out this way again, not only will I haul both of you in front of Rosenthal, but I guarantee you'll be eatin' 'taters and carrots all winter instead of elk and venison."

"This mean I don't got to go to Cody today, Sheriff?"

"Not today, Harmon."

"Appreciate it, Guy."

Guy Macauley worked his way through the clutter back to the door. Half way through, he called back to Harmon Brody.

"Hey, Harmon... me and Billy are fixin' to bring in our second cutting this weekend. We could sure use a hand if you're looking to pick up a few extra bucks."

Harmon Brody puffed out his chest. Haying was real man's work. It was also real hard work. "Let me think about it. I'll give you a call."

"Suit yourself."

Macauley climbed into his jeep and headed for Powell.

*Yaponcha started his dance, first in one direction then in another.*

*The winds had been light and variable and generally from the south-west, shepherding the fires to the northeast towards high mountain lakes and jagged rocky peaks. Then the sun rose, the thermals warmed and the wind swung around to the north.*

# Chapter Eleven

Jill Curtis finished loading the eighth horse into the second trailer just as Will Shorter and his hand pulled into the drive with his four-horse rig. He swung a big circle and backed the big blue trailer close to the corral. Jill guided him back with hand signals.

"That's good!"

Shorter and his wranglers climbed out of the F-350 Crewcab. The cowboys went right to work loading the last four horses.

"What's the game plan, Jill?"

"If you and your men can take care of Crazy Creek and Lake Creek Overlook, we can handle the rest." Jill Curtis gave Will Shorter the closest and safest trails to deal with.

"No problem. We dealing with real rangers or college kids?"

"Can't say for sure. Probably both. Luck of the draw."

"Thurston gonna just let the whole area burn?"

"I don't know. He may not have a choice. You know how fire is, Will."

"That, I surely do, sweetheart. We ready?"

Jill and the men loaded the tack into the beds of the three pickups pulling the now loaded double length horse trailers. She slapped the bed rail on the first Hunter Peak truck. "Nell, kennel!"

A blue eyed, black and white border collie raced up and scrambled over the side of the pickup into the bed. Charlie Benteen pulled out first with Harvey Rent. They would haul their horses the farthest and work the Island Lake and Beartooth Creek trails. Jill Curtis and Reno Murphy went second. They would take care of the Native Lake and Clay Butte trails, at least as far as the fire would let them. Will Shorter and his man would handle the Lake Creek Overlook and Crazy Creek trails.

Two of the trucks had powerful V-8's, the other a Cummins diesel. They would need all their power and gearing to haul their heavy loads over the mountain switchbacks. They would also need their brakes.

"Could be worse," Jill told Reno Murphy sardonically. "Could be winter."

Reno spit tobacco juice through his handlebar mustaches out the open window.

"Ain't never seed no forest fires in winter."

---

Maureen Andersen is puzzled. There is something she does not follow.

"Hold on a second, Kris. You keep talking about this Let Burn policy the Forest Service had, but I don't understand what you mean. I mean, they weren't just going to let the forest burn, were they?"

Kristian sipped her coffee then looked up from her drink. "That's exactly what they were supposed to do, at least in some areas."

Andersen was stunned. "That's crazy. Why on earth would they do a thing like that?"

Kristian smiled weakly. "That's what I thought too. I even tried to discuss it with Joshua, but he just looked at me and told me, *It wasn't the policy*. So I talked to Jon VanStavern about it, and he suggested I talk to Dr. Rolfe Johannsen at the university, who I believe was a former colleague of Leopold."

"The author, right?"

"The naturalist and author, right. Dr. Johannsen was a professor of environmental ecology. He sort of set me straight. I mean, I know you and I grew up with Smokey the Bear and *Only you can prevent forest fires*. And for a long time the prevailing view was that the only good forest fire was the one that was out or, even better, the one that didn't get started. But Dr. Johannsen explained all about how fire is just another part of nature, of certain ecosystems, just like air and soil and water. And did you know, for example, that most forest fires in wilderness areas are started by lightning? And that most only burn about a quarter of an acre, or maybe an acre or so, before they burn themselves out? And did you know, for instance, that there are some kind of pine trees, like lodgepole pine up in Wyoming, I think, that have seed cones that only open and spread their seed under extreme heat?"

"I didn't know any of that. But what about the ones you see on TV? They don't look quite as innocuous as you make them sound."

"None of them are innocuous. The ones you see on TV are the exceptions. The ones that have gotten out of hand and are threatening human life or property."

"Still, to have a policy of just letting all those trees burn. I mean, intuitively it just seems so wrong."

"Dr. Johannsen said the problem wasn't that the Forest Service wanted to let the forest burn. He said the problem was that they hadn't let it burn for a hundred years. Apparently if you don't allow forests to burn periodically, they accumulate a lot of dead trees and debris that go up like paper when they finally do catch fire. And that makes the fire spread that much faster and that much farther when it happens, especially if there is any wind."

"And I take it there was wind."

"Oh, yes, there was wind."

**Harrison:** What were the wind conditions like that day?

**Thurston:** They weren't too bad at sunup. Probably five to ten miles an hour. As the day warmed up, the wind picked up, maybe fifteen to twenty miles per hour with gusts that were higher. Later in the day it got worse, and by nightfall it was much worse.

**Baxter:** I have a report here from The National Weather Service. It states that the wind was only light in the morning and only somewhat stronger later on.

**Thurston:** Last time I looked we didn't have a National Weather Service weather station in the Beartooths. My guess is that report came from Billings or Helena.

**Baxter:** The report is from Billings, Montana, only seventy-five miles away.

**Thurston:** Mr. Baxter, seventy-five miles can make a big difference in the mountains. The mountains and gulches can create their own weather and their own wind. We figured that out after Mann Gulch. Big fires can do the same thing. My guess is that's what happened later on.

**Harrison:** Mr. Thurston, on what do you base your figures?

**Thurston:** We have a wind sock, wind gauge and barometer at the Clay Butte fire tower. I was also getting reports from the spotters in the air.

"Anybody down there, Clay Butte? This is Spirit Mountain 173."

"Hello again, Mitch."

"Hank, I'm at 13,000 feet heading 340. That outfit at Native Lake has gotten considerable bigger, maybe twenty acres. The ridge fire between Thiel and Burnt Bacon hasn't linked up yet, but I'm still guessing it will. Thiel and Upper Granite fires are still the biggest. All in all, you got well over a hundred, maybe two hundred acres burning."

"Can you tell what direction they're moving?"

"Most of the smoke's moving off to the northeast, but I gotta tell you, it's gusty up here. We're getting bounced around pretty good. Hope I remembered the baggies."

"See any people moving around?"

"Not from up here. FAA don't want me going no lower, and I'm guessing neither does my charter." Walker glanced sideways at the green face of the man sitting to his right. He suppressed a smile. "I seen those smokejumpers go in down by Native Lake when I was up here earlier an' I seen another plane down there dropping red goo. I'll fly by on my way back, like I told you, and swoop down, have another look-see."

"Think it's too windy for Rick?"

"I wouldn't want to be in one of them dang whirlybirds, but you know Rick. Rita's found him down in Gray Bull. Should be in Cody any time. Give him a call."

"I'll do that, Mitch, thanks."

"Til we meet again."

Guy Macauley waited until he reached the intersection at route 120 before trying to raise Cody on his radio. He drove his jeep onto the east shoulder just after turning north and called in.

"Good morning, Guy. How are the Brodys doing?"

"SOS, Marcia. I got the keys," he reported to the dispatcher. "Is

Mick there?"

"Heading down to Meeteetse, Guy. Said he'd be back by noon. You bringing the Brodys in?"

"Not this time, hon. They don't mean each other no harm. Probably the only bit of excitement either one of them has. Mick still want me to stop in at Powell."

"As a matter of fact, he doesn't, Guy. Not if you don't have the Brodys. Apparently there are some fires up in the Beartooths. Mick wants you to check in with Hank Thurston up at Clay Butte. See if there's anything we can do to help out."

"Clay Butte, you say?"

"You got it. Call in when you get there. I'll let Mick know you're on your way."

"Will do. Anything else?"

"That's it for now. Over."

"Over."


By 8:30 am Arthur Marshall had already ordered two drops of fire retardant: one on the fire near Native Lake; the second on the meadow southwest of Native Lake that would serve as a safety zone. Marshall was known for his liberal use of chemical retardant, the cost be damned. Sometimes he caught hell for it from the bureaucrats over him, but that never stopped him. Nor did their criticism stop him from flying down with his first team of jumpers and jumping himself, even though he was easily in his late forties. Marshall did not jump with his team at Native Lake. Instead, he flew in the C-47 to gain a first-hand view of the situation. And his solo jump near Clay Butte saved valuable time for both himself and the plane, which became the primary spotter.

Also by 8:30 all rangers were in place at their assigned trailheads and all trails in the designated sector were closed to the public.

"How do things, look, people?"

"Hank, this is Jack at Crazy Creek. We got three cars. We can see a few people on the trail. Mike's going after them now."

"Good job. Once you get them, just sit tight. I got horses and a chopper coming. We'll use the chopper to help spot hikers and direct the people on horseback. I don't expect the fires to reach you anyway."

"Hank, this is Michelle at Lake Creek Overlook. Gate closed, no cars."

"Good, just sit tight."

"This is Laura, Hank. I'm at the Beartooth Lake trailhead. We've got four cars, half a dozen tents. Can't see any people."

"Okay, Laurie, the campers can stay at the trailhead and the lake for now, but no one goes past 621. I'm going to have Rick fly over your section first. Who's at Island Lake?"

"That'd be Robbie and John."

"Okay, now Laurie, when the horses get there, I want you and the wrangler to take the trail to Grayling Lake, and then get as close to Native Lake as you can without spooking the horses. Come back along the upper trail to Beauty and then down by Crane. John, you take the Island Lake trail up to Beauty Lake and then back down to Beartooth. You got any cars?"

"Just one, two tents."

"How about Ghost Creek?"

"Negative, Hank. People usually come out here. Go in at Clay Butte."

Thurston knew this, but he was relieved to hear it all the same. "Good. Let's get people out of these areas ASAP, and keep them out. But be careful out there. These things can change direction and blow up in a second. I've called in fire teams. I want to stop this thing at the Shoshone."

Laura Miller wondered how that would sit with the bureaucrats and policy makers in D.C. Not too well was her guess.

Eric "Rick" Littlejohn was nauseous, as usual, just before his Bell 212 "Huey" helicopter lifted off shortly after nine. The loud throbbing of the rotors did not help his blinding headache one bit. The bloody Mary and two cups of black coffee he had downed after being awakened by Rita Walker had not done their jobs. It took Littlejohn fifteen minutes of flying, which put him just south of Beartooth Pass, for him to realize that it was the wind, not his hangover, that was causing his erratic flight pattern. Rick Littlejohn sobered up real fast.

"Clay Butte, this is SMA chopper 1 calling. I'm about ten miles to the east. Good morning."

"Morning, Rick. Glad you could make it."

"Not so loud, please. What can I do for you?"

"We got fire at Native Lake and north of Upper Granite Lake. We know we got some visitors in the Shoshone on this side and maybe in the Absaroka on the other, and we want to make sure they're all out if we decide to let it burn."

"You really think you have a choice?"

"I have discretion in the Shoshone, and I'll move in the Absaroka if there are people involved."

"I mean the wind, man. I don't know how it is where you're at, but I'm gettin' bounced all over the place up here. You plan on doin' any fire-fighting, you'd best get started last night."

"I've called in fire teams, and I'm sending people in on horseback to notify hikers. I need you to spot people we need to get to, talk to them if you can, pluck them out if necessary, and direct the horse people as needed to people you can't get to."

"Where you want me to start?"

"Check the immediate fire areas first. Then cover the sector between Granite Lake, Beauty Lake and here. We know we have a few people hiking around down there. Once that area is clear, we'll have you work your way west."

"That all?"

"For now."

"You don't happen to have any Dramamine down there, do you?"

"Sorry."

"Damn."

Yaponcha fanned the flames that the Great Plumed Serpent had started. Masauwu ran and danced through the tree tops. Gogyeng Sowuhti
prayed. There was nothing she could do.

The wind acted as a bellows on a hearth fire. Only there was no
hearth to contain these fires. The flames rose up and danced in the forest
crown. Then they began to run.

# Chapter Twelve

The smokejumpers in Boise, Idaho gathered up their gear: forty pounds of Nomex and hard hats, gloves and goggles, lights, batteries, water jugs and underwear all stuffed into red canvass backpacks. They were coming off only two days rest after nearly a month in Idaho fighting fires near McCall. They bitched and grumbled as they packed up for transport to Cody, Wyoming, but, like most firefighters, this was what they lived for, not to mention the five dollars per hour.

"We flying up?" Tom Harrow asked his crew boss.

"I reckon," Jess Untrup replied.

"Shit, I was countin' on a few hours shut-eye in the trucks."

"Let's get a move on. It won't get any easier if we dawdle."

"Shit, man. This is worse than 'Nam."

"You rather be there? – Let's move it ladies!"

The firefighters based at Red Lodge had had it easier that summer, but then, they were mostly irregulars or *casuals* as they were called. Not that they weren't experienced professionals. The informal designation *casuals* meant only that they weren't on the government's full-time payroll. This summer they had been called out routinely to put out spot fires, mostly in or around Yellowstone. Still, those who held down regular jobs were sick of this summer. Those without regular jobs at least had something to talk about at the local bars.

Thurston hoped to have the firefighters from Red Lodge in place west of Native Lake by eleven a.m. It was looking less and less likely that the smokejumpers from Boise would be able to jump into position, due to the increasing wind and the difficult terrain. They would most likely have to fly into Cody and then be ferried by helicopter to the fires. Hopefully, they too would be in place before noon.

"Clay Butte, this is SMA Cessna 173. I see you got Rick flying around down there. Either he's drunk as a skunk, or you got a real problem with wind."

"You tell me, Mitch."

"We got wind, Hank, and it's switchin' around. Looks like it's mostly out of the southwest, but every now and then I catch a gust out of the north, then another from the northeast. Comin' from all over, and it's stirred up them fires pretty good."

"That's what I was afraid of, Mitch. We have Rick looking for hikers and campers and directing our people on horseback. The fire crews have their own spotter. Any chance you might lend a hand too?"

"Til my tank runs dry. Where you want me to start?"

"I want you to keep an eye on the size and direction of the fires. Direct Rick to the areas most in harm's way first and let him check them out. Let me know if you spot any people down there, and we'll get to them one way or another."

"You got it, partner. Any word from your friends?"

"Not yet, but I'm sure it's just a matter of time. We've made contact with a couple of dozen people so far. I'm sure they'll show up."

"Hope so."

*Masauwu orchestrated the destruction in preparation for the trial.*

*Ground fire superheated the trees awaiting a shift in wind and a gasp of fresh air. Hundred year old trees blazed up and torched out, igniting new fires in the crown and on the forest floor.*

# Chapter Thirteen

**Harrison:** Mr. Thurston, can you explain why the smokejumpers from Boise had to fly to Cody and be ferried to the fires by helicopter? Why didn't they just parachute down in the area of the fires like the Missoula team did? Wouldn't that have put them in place a lot sooner?

**Thurston:** My understanding is that the winds were too high and too unpredictable for a safe jump. Is that right, Arthur?"

**Harrison:** Mr. Marshall, would you care to elaborate?

**Fire Supervisor Arthur Marshall:** Yes, sir. Mr. Thurston is correct. We judged the winds to be fifteen to twenty miles per hour by the time the Boise team arrived, borderline for a jump in ideal circumstances, not in the mountains. There were also erratic gusts of wind in excess of twenty to twenty-five miles per hour. That made it a no brainer.

**Carton:** Isn't that what your men are

trained to do, sir, jump under difficult conditions?

**Marshall**: Difficult? Yes. Suicidal? No. Even if the wind hadn't been gusting and we had decided to jump in, we would have had to pick a jump zone so far from the fire it would have taken the team a good half day or more to gather their gear and get into place.

**Carton**: I don't understand.

**Marshall**: No, sir, you don't. Look, just because a spot on a topo map looks close to another spot, that don't make it so. A half mile as the crow flies can mean a whole day trek if you're on the wrong side of a damn mountain. The only good jump zones in the vicinity of the fires would have required absolute ideal conditions, not twenty-five mile per hour winds. Understand now?

**Carton**: I don't care for your tone, Mr. Marshall.

**Marshall**: And I don't care for a bunch of paper pushers and arm chair quarterbacks second guessing the men on the ground.

The luck of the draw put Laura Miller on a strawberry Appaloosa, paired up with Reno Murphy on his white stockinged black. They walked their horses through the campground, to the envy of several campers thinking they were just out for a morning trail ride. They picked up the trail at the north end of the campground and contained their horses, agitated by the wind. They continued to walk the quarter mile to the junction of trails 619 and 621. Once on 619, Miller and Murphy let their mounts ease into a quick trot and occasional canter as they circumvented the northern perimeter of Beartooth Lake and headed west towards the 10,500 foot Beartooth Butte. The early going was easy, across open terrain that was normally wet and boggy but that this year was dry and dusty. When they turned north again the trail began to climb. Forest was visible winding around the north end of the butte, lodgepole pine and whitebarks mostly, but this area was pretty safe from fire, even in a dry year. Their job was just to make certain no hikers inadvertently walked into harm's way.

Rick Littlejohn flew overhead, performing an unintentional sky dance as he tried to hold a line.

"Rangers, I got three, no, make that four, maybe five hikers heading north on the east side of Beartooth Butte. Looks like they're heading for the woods. I may not be able to catch them before they get there. Over."

"We see them up ahead," Laura radioed back. "We'll take care of them. Over."

"You got 'em. Have fun."

Reno Murphy spit tobacco juice and kicked up his horse.

*Joshua and Vanstavern sit quietly in the wood heated kitchen, drinking whisky and coffee.* Joshua was dog tired. His body still ached from the horrible three day ordeal in Vermont from which he had just returned. He had a low-grade headache at the base of his skull. He wasn't sure if it came from his sore, exhausted muscles or from the fear and stress he always felt when he thought about that night out in Wyoming.

"According to Mick Dugan, Guy Macauley was a pretty good

deputy," Jonathan began.

Joshua hesitated before answering. He had never really discussed the details of the Wyoming rescue with anybody before, not on a personal level. He was reluctant to do so now. *What the hell, he thinks, if I'm gonna get past it with Kristian, I'd better get past it with Jon.*

"Good deputy, good man."

"Mick said he played double-A ball straight out of high school, before he got drafted and sent to 'Nam."

"Yeah, that's what I heard. I figured he was some kind of athlete from the way he moved and the way he carried himself. I just didn't know what kind."

"You never told me that he saved your life."

"I never told anybody much of anything about that damn night, except that damn Board of Review."

"Not even Macauley's family?"

Joshua looked sternly at his old friend. "Yeah, I guess I told them."

---

*Guy Macauley turns onto the dirt road that leads to the Clay Butte overlook and drives his jeep to the parking area.* Before hopping out, he reached between the seats and dug out a pair of binoculars. Macauley stood in his vehicle, straddling the driver's seat and bracing himself against the roll bar as he surveyed the situation in the distance. He let out a long, low whistle. Then the deputy sheriff walked to the gate and spoke with Richie Volas.

"How's it going?"

"Not too bad, I think. We got things closed off and we're getting people out. Hank's called in some teams. I think one team of smoke-jumpers is in place already and others are on the way."

"Thought you had a new policy?"

"We do, but it's only mandatory in designated areas. I guess Hank's got some wiggle room in the Shoshone, and he's decided not to let things get out of hand, what with things being so dry and all."

Macauley nodded. He scanned the area one more time with his binoculars, then he climbed the metal stairs of the lookout tower. He found the supervising ranger standing by the screen window, watching the situation develop to the north.

"Howdy, Hank."

Thurston turned, momentarily surprised. "Well, howdy, Guy. Didn't expect to see you up here."

"Mick wanted me to take a look-see. Wants to know if there's anything we can do."

"Don't think so, Guy. Not at the moment. I think I've got things pretty well covered. As long as we can keep things from moving south or west I think we'll be all right."

"Blowin' around pretty good out there. Richie said you called in some teams."

"Yeah."

"You gonna get into trouble for that?"

"Maybe. I don't think so though. They want it both ways. Let it burn as long as it don't endanger life or property. I reckon that gives me some discretion."

Macauley nodded silently.

"Need any help getting people out?"

Hank Thurston turned back to the scene in the north. He considered the situation on the ground, and he considered Macauley's offer. Then he thought about his friends.

"I wouldn't mind having another chopper up there. I'm not sure what kind of shape Rick's in, and he's got a lot of ground to cover."

Macauley understood. He knew Rick Littlejohn. He had arrested him three times for drunk and disorderly.

"There's a team of biologists in the area somewhere too, a family, friends of mine actually, and I'll feel a whole lot better once I know they're out."

"I'll call Cody 'n have Mick send Jack up."

Thurston checked his watch.

"Mick said the chopper wouldn't be up before noon."

"I'll call all the same. Maybe they can speed things up."

Thurston looked over at Macauley. "I'd appreciate it."

Toward the north end of Beartooth Butte, Laura Miller and Reno Murphy caught up with the group of day hikers just inside the tree line.

"Good morning."

"Good morning. Nice horses."

"Nice day for a ride. Might be getting a little warm though."

"Good morning, folks," Laura Miller returned. "I'm afraid this area is closed. You'll have to turn back."

"No one said anything to us. What's the problem?" the professor leading the field trip inquired.

"We've got some fires in the area. We need this area clear."

"How close are the fires?"

Reno Murphy perked up. He thought he heard a challenge in the question. It would be interesting to see how Miller handled it.

"Two, three miles away. Native Lake area. You can see the smoke."

"Looks like clouds to me."

"Smoke."

"Well, we'll be careful." The university professor was secretly pleased. With luck, he would have a rare, first hand opportunity to teach his students about the true nature of fire and its place in forest ecology. His peers and his students would be impressed, especially the co-eds. "We're just hiking over to Claw Lake and then down around Beauty Lake on the way back. I don't think we'll have any problems, do you?"

"The problem you have is that the area is closed. You need to turn around and you need to do it now," Miller told them calmly.

"We'll assume all responsibility, Ranger."

With that, the party of five hikers began to continue on its way. Miller did not hesitate, not even to check with Murphy. She spurred her horse ahead of the hikers and blocked the trail.

"Now, I'm going to tell you one more time, and just one more time. You need to turn around and go back to the campground."

"And if we don't?"

"As a ranger of the United States Forest Service I am also a deputy U.S. marshal in declared emergency areas. This area is a declared emergency area. If you do not cooperate, you will be placed under arrest."

The leader of the hikers looked resentfully at Miller. Then he looked at Murphy.

"I suppose you're a deputy marshal too?"

Murphy spit. "Nope. Deputy sheriff, Park County, Wyoming." With that Murphy withdrew a shiny silver six pointed star from his shirt pocket and pinned it to his jacket.

Faced with the possibility of arrest, not to mention re-evaluation of the male students' draft classifications, the hikers reconsidered and turned around.

Miller radioed Littlejohn.

"Rick, keep an eye on those hikers on 619, will you? I just want to make sure they keep heading back to camp."

"Roger, Laurie. Will do."

Laura Miller and Reno Murphy continued on the trail north-northwest towards Native Lake.

"You really a deputy sheriff, Mr. Murphy?"

"Nope."

"Where'd you get the badge?"

"Cooper's Souvenir Store in Cook City." Murphy spit again as he reined his horse over. "Kids get a kick outta them. Give 'em out after trail rides. Usually buy 'em by the gross."

Miller smiled to herself. She was satisfied with her draw.

So was Murphy. After a few minutes chewing, he asked the ranger, "You really a deputy U.S. marshal?"

"Hell no."

*By noon the fire had doubled in size. More than three hundred and fifty acres were burning. That number increased rapidly.*

# Chapter Fourteen

As the firefighters from Red Lodge wound their way up and around Beartooth Pass, the smokejumpers from Boise were airborne, heading northeast in a thirty-year-old surplus C-47. Also on the way was a second DC-6 retardant plane carrying six thousand pounds of chemical retardant.

As in the military, jumpers only jumped when there was no better alternative. It was often easier, safer, and more efficient to be ferried to a site by helicopter. In this case the chopper was a Sikorski HT 171 that would also be used to drop water ladled out of Granite Lake by a seven hundred-gallon dipper suspended from the frame of the aircraft. The water wouldn't extinguish the fire, but with luck it would slow things down enough to give the firefighters time to clear a break. The Sikorski that would be used for this fire was a five-year-old outfit leased by the Forest Service from the Peter Teller Construction Company in Jackson Hole, Wyoming. It was rigged with the retractable dipper and would meet the jumpers at Cody.

The Red Lodge teams checked in with Hank Thurston at Clay Butte at 9:49 a.m.

"Where do you want us, Mr. Thurston?" Fred Jenkins, the crew foreman, inquired.

"You're going to reinforce the Missoula team. I want a line formed south and west of Native Lake. If we catch a break from the wind, we might be able to direct this thing north and east."

There was considerably less fuel northeast of Native Lake due to the geology of the peaks in that direction. There was also a string of small lakes, ponds, bogs and streams in that area. If the Native Lake fire could be encouraged in that direction it would fizzle and burn itself out in short order.

"Where you going to have the Boise team?"

"Good question. Somewhere around Park Rapids, I'm guessing. We'll see what the situation looks like when they get here. Let me know if you need backup, and make damn sure you have safe zones. Don't want no Mann Gulch."

"No shit. How you want us to go in?"

"Probably easiest to drive the jeep trail by Muddy Creek and as far in on 568 as you can. You'll have to hoof it in once you get to 618," Thurston explained, going over the map with the strike leaders.

"Right. Guess that's about it. What's your frequency?"

"118.6. One other thing, Fred..."

"Yeah...?"

"Keep an eye out for any hikers. We got people moving them out and choppers spotting, but you never know."

"Sure thing. Talk to you later."

"Later, yeah. Call when you're in place."

"Will do."

"Good luck."

"Yeah, you too."

Gogyeng Sowuhti had seen Masauwu work before. She knew what he was capable of and she was frightened. She was frightened for the Son of Light and she was frightened for White Wind. And she was frightened for the others.

The advancing front of an active forest fire is one of the most dangerous places on earth. Some say it's the flames and the heat that makes things so bad, some say it's the lack of oxygen and the noxious gasses. Still others hold it's the blinding, choking smoke and the crashing tree limbs. Truth be told, what really makes a forest fire so dangerous is the unpredictability of the situation. In 1949 sixteen smokejumpers learned about the unpredictability of an active wildfire at a place called Mann Gulch.

# Chapter Fifteen

*In the Irish tavern in San Francisco Maureen Anderson sits mesmer-*
*ized by Kristian's revelations.*

"This is an amazing story," Andersen commented. "So one of the rangers was a woman?"

"Yes, Laura Miller. One of the first full-time women rangers in the nation."

"Interesting. That's the second time you've mentioned Mann Gulch, Kris. What was Mann Gulch?"

Kristian was back to drinking coffee. She sipped the hot black beverage from the chipped white restaurant cup. The dinner crowd had cleared out, for the most part, and the restaurant was feeling empty. Dishes being washed and stacked rattled though the kitchen door. Then she answered.

"I asked the same question after I first read the transcript be-cause it came up more than once. I had to do some research, but I finally found out. It's a place in the Helena National Forest along the Missouri River in western Montana. In 1949 thirteen smokejump-ers were killed on their way to fight what they thought was just a routine fire."

"My God! How did that happen? If they were on their way to the fire, why on earth didn't they just turn around and leave if there was a problem?"

"They tried. It wasn't so simple. The wind shifted, the terrain was difficult, the fire changed direction, and they couldn't outrun it. Only three men survived, two who outran it and one who burned a patch of grass ahead of him and then lay down in the ashes and let the main fire pass over and around him."

"You've got to be kidding. How on earth could he do that?"

"I don't know, but he did. There was a Board of Review after that fire too. The Forest Service changed some of their policies, and..."

"What kind of policy changes did they make?"

"I don't know exactly. I think they realized the necessity for better defined safe areas that would facilitate evacuation if necessary. And I think they learned the importance of redundancy, you know, backup equipment and safety areas. Most importantly, I think they learned that smokejumpers weren't invincible."

"Clay Butte, this is Park County Sheriff's Department Chopper 212-1. I'm ten minutes out. What can I do for you?"

"Howdy, Jack. Glad you could make it. We've got Rick Littlejohn covering sections R105W and R106W. If you can handle R106W west of Muddy Creek, then Rick can stay between Native Lake and Granite."

"No problem. What you want me to do?"

"Look for hikers and campers. Make sure they're heading back to the trailheads. Talk to them if you feel you need to and you can do it safely, otherwise direct our people on horseback to the people you can't get to. Shouldn't be too many. And let us know if you spot any new fires. How's the wind up there?"

"Terrible. Gets any worse and I might have to set her down. How's Rick doing?"

"Not pretty, but he's getting the job done."

"Think he's drunk?"

"Doubt it. Hangover, maybe, but I doubt he's drunk. Anyway, he's getting it done."

"Roger that. How you want me to direct your people."

"118.6. You can talk to them directly. We're monitoring all traffic."

"118.6 Lock. Anything else?"

"Just use your own judgment, Jack. If it gets too rough up there then get out. I told that to Littlejohn too, but you know Rick."

"Yeah, I know Rick. Talk to you later."

"You bet."

"You're back early," the Park County sheriff's dispatcher observed as Mick Dugan walked into the office.

"Nothing heavy down in Meeteetse. Mayor wanted input on a few matters. Guy bring in the Brodys?"

"Not this time. Said he got the keys, though."

Dugan smiled and nodded. "You send him up to Clay Butte?"

"Sure did. Sounds like they've got things pretty much under control. Jack's up there now too."

"Good. Anything else Hank needs from us?"

"Don't think so. Guy said he was heading down to Hunter Peak. Probably bum some lunch if I know him. Wants to know what you want him to do next."

"Have him patrol the northwest corner, make himself available to Thurston if he needs him."

"Yes, sir."

The Red Lodge teams drove in as far as they could without risking their vehicles. It was farther in than any of them would have ever thought possible. The open meadow that began at the end of the one mile jeep road was always too wet and too boggy to be traversed by any wheeled vehicle. This year it was hardscrabble dry, which saved the hotshots and casuals nearly three miles of walking. But the firefighters still had to hike, single file, a good half-mile over rough terrain, packing thirty to forty pounds of gear and equipment before they were in place.

Their goal was to widen the north-south trail, number 618, enough so the Native Lake fire couldn't jump it if the winds shifted to the northeast. They would also widen an unofficial, but clearly delineated, trail that ran east and west and that connected trail 618 with trail 568. They had several escape routes, and their fall-back position would be the meadow at the junction of 568 and 618.

"Ain't never seen it so dry. You, Fred?" Kyle Manning remarked to the foreman.

"No, I haven't."

"Better keep in touch with them spotters. These trees ain't much more'n kindlin' wood. Day like today an' a good fire could jump anywheres, an' fast."

"Count on it." Fred Jenkins knew enough to heed any advice Manning might offer. Manning was one of those experienced standards found on fire crews who didn't seem to have an ounce of ambition pertaining to anything other than fighting fires. Then he was a man in his element who knew his stuff. Jenkins was a pro, but he wouldn't hesitate to consult Manning.

"We got any red goo comin'?"

"Already been some. Supposed to get more."

Manning nodded. He stretched as he got out of his pack and fired up his twenty-four inch Homelite chain saw. He looked around before he commenced to cutting his first lodgepole pine.

"Hope it gets here right quick," he said to no one in particular.

The screen door slammed behind Guy Macauley as he entered the Hunter Peak lodge that connected to the dining area. He smiled as he looked over at the fieldstone fireplace with the authentic Henry-Hawkings muzzle loader still mounted at the same jaunty angle it had always been. The elk racks were still spaced along the wall, as were the mule deer racks and hides. Macauley thought he noticed one four-point he did not remember. One black bearskin was also on the wall. It was the same fine place he had known and loved most of his life, kept up by the same fine people. Macauley strode through the door that connected the lodge to the dining room. He walked up beside Sandra Curtis, pouring lemonade at the serving table, and slipped his hand around her waist.

"Why Guy Macauley, as I live and breathe. Where've you been keeping yourself, boy?"

"Talk to Mick Dugan. You know if it was up to me I'd be living up here."

"Can always use another hand. Think Jan'll go for it?"

"Hmm. Could be a problem there. Probably wouldn't be a problem so long as Jill's at vet school in Idaho."

Guy Macauley and Jill Curtis had been good friends most of their lives, despite a four year age difference. Guy's father and Roy Curtis had been friends, and Guy's dad started bringing Guy to Hunter Peak from the time he could walk. When Matt Macauley was killed in Korea the Curtis family practically adopted Guy. Guy and Jill periodically attended the same schools together, either in Powell or in Cody. But it was their love of the outdoors, of horses and of dogs, of hunting and of fishing, and of the guest ranch nestled in the shadow of its namesake mountain that forged Guy and Jill into fast, lifelong friends.

At one time, Sandy Curtis thought she might have Guy Macauley for a son-in-law. That thought may even have crossed Jill and Guy's minds too after Guy graduated from high school. But Guy had met Janice Heath while playing double-A ball in Jackson. Then came his hitch in the Army. He had volunteered to serve as an advisor before most people knew where Vietnam was. By the time he returned from overseas he had a three-year-old son. It was just as well. Jill had just started college. Having a family was the last thing on her mind. They still remained good friends.

"Jill's up in the Shoshone with some of the hands, helping Hank Thurston clear the trails of tourists."

"I know. I just come from Clay Butte."

"How things going up there?"

"Hard to say. Hank seems to have things under control, but the wind is pretty stiff and tricky. And you know what kind of a summer it's been."

"That I do. You want some lunch?"

"Have enough?"

Sandra Curtis gave Macauley her *what-kind-of-a-dumb-ass-question-is-that* look. "And don't go digging around for your wallet like you're going to pay. You haven't paid for a meal here in twenty-eight years, and I don't expect you're about to start now."

"If you insist," Macauley smiled.

"Hank heard anything from the Barstows?"

"Those the biologist friends of his out taggin' bears."

"Yes. They're guests here. Come up every year."

"Not that I know of."


By twelve-thirty p.m. the Sikorski had the Boise team in place northwest of Park Rapids. Bureaucratic decree dictated that the smokejumpers stay south of the Montana border, where the Absoroka Beartooth Wilderness officially began. But the bureaucrats weren't on the ground. The firefighters began clearing a handline on the south bank of the dried up stream bed that almost connected North Hidden Lake with Upper Granite Lake. If possible, they would also cut a break between the creek and Thiel Lake. Ten men, half the team, carried water bladders on their backs. They would be filled from the remnants of the small lake and used to douse any stray embers that drifted in. The goal was to prevent the wildfires burning in the wilderness area from linking up with those in the Shoshone. The problem was that they needed dozers, loaders and backhoes. All they had were chainsaws, shovels, pulaskis and mcleods.

The increasing winds were beginning to play havoc with the fires on the ground and the helicopters in the air. The larger lake surfaces were chopped with whitecaps. The Sikorski ladled up its first bucket of water from Granite Lake with much more difficulty than anticipated. Harder still was dropping the load accurately.

When the seven hundred-gallon payload hit the raging fire, the water vaporized instantly into a cloud of steam. The effect it had on the fire was negligible.

The Missoula and Red Lodge teams, farther to the south, weren't fairing much better. Just when they thought they were making progress, the wind would shift, and they would have to retreat. The load of chemical retardant, a slurried mixture of water, red clay and fertilizer, appropriately dubbed *red goo*, arrived at 1:30 p.m., delivered by a converted DC-6.

Flying south through high gusting cross winds was tricky enough. Threading its way at low altitude between parallel mountain ridges was damn near impossible, even with a lead plane. When the plane dropped its load, some of the retardant drifted on or behind the fire team.

"Goddamn goo!" Manning shouted to the sky. "You're supposed to drop the shit on the goddamn fire!"

After lunch, Guy Macauley patrolled southeast on highway 296, The Chief Joseph Highway. He stopped by the North Crandall general store, bought a Dr. Pepper and drove the narrow lanes of the trailer park located there. Macauley let people know about the fire, even though the park probably wasn't in any danger and most everybody had already heard. Still, Macauley knew, it didn't hurt for these folks to see a friendly face every once and a while, especially one that went with a badge.

Macauley continued his cruise of the scenic road, with its long, steep grades and hairpin curves, as far as Dead Indian Pass. Then he turned around and headed back. He looked out over the Sunlight Basin and decided maybe it wouldn't be a bad idea to check in at home. The deputy sheriff wheeled his jeep left, onto the dry and dusty Sunlight Creek Road, and headed for his ranch.

Driving the Creek Road down from the Chief Joseph was one of the perks of the job that always kept Macauley fresh. To his way of thinking, this valley was the most beautiful place on earth. Not many would take issue with him. Each time Guy Macauley rounded the last bend and first spied the cedar log buildings that were his homestead his heart swelled with joy, and he felt a satisfaction and contentment known to few men.

"Daddy!" little Annie cried with joy, jumping up from her game and racing to her father who scooped her up in his arms as he had that morning.

"Howdy, Pumpkin. Now where on earth did you find mud this time of year?" Once again, the deputy's clothes were soiled.

"The crick."

Mud was about all there was in the creek this year.

"Where's Billy?"

"Swimmin'"

"He take Cisco, or he ride his bike?"

Cisco was the boy's horse.

"He rode his bike. He took Jimmy."

Jimmy was their yellow Lab.

Macaluley nodded as he looked around, still holding Annie in his arms.

"Where's momma?"

"Hangin' wash."

"And you're not helping her? Shame on you."

"She said I didn't have to. I'm too dirty," Annie proclaimed proudly. "And I rode Jasper." Jasper was her pony.

"Good for you, Pumpkin. Now, down you go."

Macauley smiled as he placed his daughter gently on the ground. The two of them walked around the house, hand-in-hand, in search of Jan Macauley. They found her hanging bedclothes on the lines behind the house, humming happily to herself. She did not hear her husband and daughter come up behind her, and she started when Guy placed his hands on her waist. Then she looked back at him and smiled.

"Dryer broke again?"

"No. I just like the way things smell when they're fresh-air dried."

"Kinda windy, ain't it?"

"I'm just hanging the bed clothes. They'll stay put, and they'll be dry in no time."

Macauley smiled. He too like the way things smelled when they were dried outside, although he would never admit it.

"Don't wait dinner for me. I might be a little late."

"Trouble?" Jan Macauley's smile faded.

"No, not really. Got a couple of fires up in the Absaroka. One this side of the line. Hank Thurston might need a little help with some of the tourists. That's all. Can you and Billy handle the chores?"

"We always do."

"Just don't want you overdoing it, is all."

"And now why is that?" Jan Macauley smiled coyly.

Guy Macauley looked into his wife's eyes.

"No reason."

She knew why. And now Guy knew also.

*Gogyeng Sowuhti pleaded with Masauwu. She pleaded with Yaponcha. She pleaded with the Great Plumed Serpent. "You know he is the Son of Light. Do not do these things."*

*Masauwu and Yaponcha and the Great Plumed Serpent heard her pleas, but they did not heed them.*

*Ground fires are often containable, especially if the wind and the terrain are on your side. Crown fires are another story, and the weather conditions and forest conditions assured that any ground fires would quickly become crown fires. Once a fire becomes a crown fire you need more than wind and terrain on your side. You also need God on your side.*

# Chapter Sixteen

**Harrison:** Just so the record is clear, Mr. Thurston, you had one helicopter and one spotter plane?

**Thurston:** No, sir. We got our first read from Mitch Walker in his Cessna. Then the C-47 that dropped the smokejumpers became a second spotter. Actually, the C-47 became the primary spotter. We had one chopper up before nine and a second up before noon. And the plane that ferried in the Boise team relieved the Missoula plane so they could refuel. We also had two choppers dropping water and moving people. And two choppers spotting hikers and giving us additional reads on the fires.

**Harrison:** Then what happened?

**Thurston:** Once the Boise team was in place, we thought we were in pretty good shape. Then around two-thirty, three o'clock things began to change.

By 2:30 p.m. the mounted rangers and volunteers had made

contact with 42 hikers, fishermen and campers. By 3:00, no more civilian personnel had been seen by the spotter planes, either of the two helicopters, or the horse riders. Then something unexpected happened. The wind swung around to the northeast. Swung around to the northeast and then shifted again to the north.

"Clay Butte, this is Park County Chopper 1. It's getting pretty hairy up here. Haven't seen anyone for over half an hour. I'm guessing we've got 'em all. If it's all the same to you, I'm headin' for home. Maybe it's just the wind, but I don't like the feel of the rudder. I'll gas up in Cody and come back at dusk if the winds settle down."

"Your call, Jack. Thanks for the help. What about you, Rick?"

"Don't have to twist my arm, Hank. I'm a headin' for the barn."

"Mitch?"

"I've got enough fuel for another hour or so. I'll see what it's like up around fifteen thousand feet. I don't like the way them fires are jumping around. I'll backup the spotter."

"Appreciate it, Mitch. Team leaders, you copy?"

"We copy, Clay Butte," Fred Jenkins returned.

"Copy," Jess Untrup called in. "Give us some warning if you think we need to move or if our safety zones are threatened, will you? It's godawful dry down here."

"Ditto here, Clay Butte."

"We'll do our best, but don't wait for us. You men know what you're doing. If you think it's time to high-tail it, get the hell out of there."


Rick Littlejohn eased back on the collective and swung the stick around to the left. He flew out over Granite Lake near the line, heading due south for a moment, then southeast, trying to locate and follow 568 and the Muddy Creek trail as best he could. Just south of the 618 fork, where the forest opens into broad meadow, Littlejohn spotted something moving.

"Hank, this is Rick, I got someone heading south on Muddy Creek, no wait, he's heading up to Clay Butte. Looks like he's really hauling the mail. You want me to have a word with him?"

"Can you put down safely?"

"Pretty steep, but I can try. He's movin' the right direction... wait a minute, he's stopped now. He's wavin' me in. Something ain't right."

"Check it out if you can, Rick. Matthew, Jill, you in the area?"

"We're about a half mile up on 618, heading home."

"Keep an eye out in case Rick can't put down."

"Got it. We're on the way."

"Almost there, now," Littlejohn reported. "I think I can put down if I can find a good cairn."

The mountain meadow was open but steep. Littlejohn had to be careful where he put down or he would not be able to lift off again. His plan was to put at least one runner on a broad flat rock in order to keep his helicopter reasonably level. As he swung around, looking for a place to land, he realized something he had not noticed before.

"Holy shit, Hank, it's a girl! And it looks like she's totin' a rifle."

But Rick Littlejohn was wrong. It was not a girl. It was a woman. Dr. Carolyn Barstow.


Carolyn Barstow raced the fifty yards east, along the contour of the meadow, to the flat spot Littlejohn had chosen to land his helicopter. All she could think was, *Thank God!*

"Please, you've got to help us!" she shouted above the loud beating of the rotors still winding down.

It wasn't enough. Littlejohn removed his headset as he opened the door for the excited woman.

"Say again, ma'am?"

This time the woman shouted directly into the pilot's ear.

"My children are missing, somewhere north of the border, north of Park Rapids!"

Littlejohn nodded. He had a lot of questions. "Get in," was all he told her.

As Carolyn Barstow scrambled off the cairn and around the front of the chopper her peripheral vision caught something to the north. It confirmed her worst fears.

"Oh, my God!"

The woman felt a dull, piercing pain in her abdomen. She thought she might lose control of her bowels. She knew she had to hold it together.

"Where are the fires?" Barstow asked of the columns of smoke she could now see for the first time.

"Got one west of Thiel Lake, and another about a mile and a half northwest of that," Littlejohn answered as he revved up his rotors and began to lift off. "Then there's another one over by Native Lake. How old are your kids, ma'am?"

"My daughter's eighteen, my son is sixteen."

That was something, Littlejohn thought, if they had any experience in the woods. Then, instead of increasing the throttle to continue the ascent, Littlejohn eased off and placed the chopper back on the cairn."

Barstow looked over to the pilot.

"What are you doing?"

"Be right back."

The pilot ran around to the blind side of his aircraft. He dry heaved for a moment and then urinated. But that wasn't the reason he re-landed his aircraft. Not far below, coming out of the woods, Littlejohn had spotted two horses with riders. He jogged down the steep meadow to meet them. Uncharacteristically, he did not wait for introductions.

"We got two teenagers missing north of Park Rapids, probably over the line. Y'all haven't come acrost 'em by any chance?"

Jill and Matthew looked at each other.

"Haven't seen anyone along 618."

"Can y'all help look? I'm gonna fly over the area, but I can't see much under the canopy and I'm running low on fuel."

The horses and riders had been working for almost five hours, much of it in ninety-plus degree heat. The horses were lathered and the riders were sweat dry. They might get water at a pond back north, but they had just come down grade and now they would have to turn around and go back up. Worst of all, once in the woods and shielded from the wind, the bugs were frightful.

Matthew looked to Jill. They were her horses.

"Sure," Jill told him without a smile. "We can try and make the loop again. C'mon, Nell. This way." The border collie looked quizzical for a second then raced to regain the lead.

"Your radios working?"

"So far. Just changed batteries."

"Okay," Littlejohn told them, "we'll keep in touch through Clay Butte."

The riders nodded and reined their horses around. Rick Littlejohn scrambled back up grade to his waiting chopper and Carolyn Barstow.

He puked one more time before climbing on board, just for luck.

"Hank, you there? This is Rick. We got us a situation."

"What's the problem, Rick?"

"Woman I picked up got separated from her kids up north of Park Rapids. I'm gonna overfly the area again, and I asked Jill Curtis and that ranger she's with to recheck the trails."

"What's the woman's name, Rick?"

"Barstow, Carolyn Barstow."

"Let me talk with her, Rick."

Littlejohn reached over and tapped Carolyn Barstow on the shoulder. "He wants to talk to you," the pilot informed his passenger, indicating the second headset on the copilot's side.

"Hello...."

"Carolyn? It's Hank Thurston."

"Oh, Hank, thank God. I feel like such a damn fool."

"What's the situation?"

"God, I wish I knew. The kids went off to get some berries for breakfast. That was around eight o'clock, but they didn't have to go far, just the meadow north of that pond along the trail. It's less than a mile east from our camp. But that's the last we've seen of them. Something's got to be wrong. You know my kids. They've got better orientation and woods-smarts than we do."

Hank Thurston did know the Barstow kids, Laura and Carl. He knew that they were more experienced and better woodsmen than many people twice their age. Carolyn was right. If they were missing from camp, something had to be wrong.

"Where's Craig?"

"He's still searching the area. We split up around noon so I could go for help."

"Rick, how you doing on fuel?"

"Runnin' on fumes. I'm gonna have to head for the barn right soon."

"Carolyn, any guesses which way they might have headed?"

"Not a clue. We caught up with Sophie and her cubs last night. And this morning, when we were looking for the kids down near the pond, we saw signs of them again, and maybe a boar."

"So you think maybe the bears got between them and camp and they had to high-tail it around?"

"It's a real possibility, Hank, and the only thing I can think of. God, Hank, how bad are the fires?"

"Not too bad at this time. We've got crews working them. Listen, Rick, can you drop Carolyn off here on your way in?"

"No problem, Hank. Should be there in ten."

"I'd rather you let me off near my camp. Maybe Craig's found them. If not, he'll need my help."

"I need you here, Carolyn. I'm going to try to get a tracking team out there, but I need you here to show us exactly where your camp is." It wasn't an outright lie, but Hank Thurston wanted Carolyn Barstow out of the woods.

"Ain't no good place to land you up here anyways, not near your camp, leastwise."

"You can put down in the meadow near our camp."

"Not in these winds."

"You come on in with Rick, Carolyn. We'll get Craig and your kids."

"Are you sure?"

Thurston thought for a moment. "Yeah," he told her, "I'm sure."

**Harrison:** In other words, it wasn't until after three p.m. that you located Mrs. Barstow and learned that there was a problem in the area of the fires.

**Thurston:** Yes, sir. Three-fourteen to be exact.

**Harrison:** What did you do next.

**Thurston:** I told Rick Littlejohn to bring Dr. Barstow to Clay Butte. Then I contacted the spotters and asked them to help with the search for the missing people.

**Baxter:** Did they?

**Thurston:** Yes, sir. Littlejohn also asked Jill Curtis and Matt Hunter if they could go back up trail and help.

**Baxter:** And did they?

**Thurston:** Yes, sir.

**Harrison:** Then what?
**Thurston:** I contacted Sheriff Dugan's office.
**Carton:** With the intention of passing off the search to him?
**Thurston:** With the intention of getting the best damn dogs and the best damn dog handler in Wyoming involved in the search, you bet your ass.

Supervising Ranger Thurston wasn't really sure about anything at that moment except that he was going to do everything in his power to find his friends' kids and evacuate them. He pondered the situation for one moment, then he swung into action and called Cody.

"Mattie, patch me into the sheriff's office, will you?"

"Sure thing, Hank. Just give me a minute..."

"Sheriff's office," the dispatcher answered.

"Marcie, this is Hank Thurston. Is Mick there?"

"He's still at the courthouse, Mr. Thurston. I expect him any time."

"Is there any way for me to get a hold of him. I got kind of an emergency up here."

"I can have him paged over there. They can get a message to him even if he's still in court."

"Why don't you do that, please. Tell Mick to call me ASAP. I'm up at the Clay Butte tower. Best thing for him to do is go through our Cody office."

"I'll get right on it, Mr. Thurston. Do you want to hold?"

"No. Just have Mick call me as soon as he can. It's urgent. Tell him to break in even if I'm on the horn."

"Yes, sir. Right away."

Thurston changed frequencies and contacted the fire-fighting teams.

"Fred, Jess, how's it look on the ground?"

"So far, so good." The supervisor had to shout into the radio to be heard above the whining chainsaws and the clanks and clunks of shovels and pulaskis. Someone yelled, *Bump!* and the line shifted west a yard. "Stream bed's pretty dry, but we've widened it for almost a quarter of a mile. We're working on the trail now," Untrup reported.

"How much you got burning?"

"Have to ask the spotters. We can smell it, but we can't see it, which is all right with me."

"How about it, HiFly1? You copy?"

"We make out about a hundred and sixty to a hundred and eighty acres in the gulch northwest of Granite Lake, south of Burnt Bacon, and about a hundred acres just northwest of Thiel. Wouldn't be surprised if they linked up. The Native Lake fire looks about half that size. The good news is the wind and topography are working with us, at least as far as Shoshone is concerned."

The wind had swung back again to southwest, and the fires were burning uphill. With any luck they would continue burning towards the Absaroka wilderness, north of the state line, where they would be contained by the bare, rocky slopes and an inordinate number of high mountain lakes. Granite Lake and the trails around it would halt any fire heading towards it, and the Native Lake chain might even prevent that fire from reaching the border. All in all, it wasn't too bad. Now if Thurston could just find those kids.

"How about your team, Fred?"

"We've cleared and widened 618 for about twenty-five hundred feet. We're working south and hope to link up them two streams before night fall."

"Sounds good. Tell the men good job. Now listen up. There's a chance we might have a couple of lost teenagers and their dad wandering around in your sectors, especially yours, Jess. Tell your men to keep an eye out, and contact me if you happen to run into them."

"What the hell they doing out here."

"Long story. They're experienced people, even the kids, but I want them out."

"No shit."

"Just give a holler if you see them."

"Roger that."

"Will do."

*Gogyeng Sowuhti called upon Red Hawk and Gray Hawk and Dog Man. She called upon the Horse People, "You must search for the children. You must help the Son of Light."*

*Ground fires tend to run fast. Crown fires run slow but intense. But on this day and in these mountains the wind and the topography, the abundance of fuel and the lack of humidity assured the worst of both worlds. Exploding crowns and popping sparks ignited raging ground fires through bone dry debris. Racing flames from the bone dry debris ignited huge trees leading to the explosions and torch-outs in the crowns.*

*The cycle continued. The areas affected by the fires expanded exponentially.*

# Chapter Seventeen

Mick Dugan was located in the first row of oak pew-like bench seats in courtroom D of the Park County Courthouse. He sat just behind the prosecutor's table, manned by John Barrett and Mike Churiello. The blue uniformed bailiff approached from the center aisle and handed him a folded note. Dugan read the note, then leaned across the three-foot high slatted oak partition and tapped the assistant prosecutor on the right shoulder.

"You still need me?"

"I don't. I don't know about Coughlin. Why, what's up?"

"Not sure. Got a message from Hank Thurston. Some kind of problem up there."

The prosecutor looked up at the wall clock and then over at James Coughlin, the defense attorney just about to call his final witness.

"Let's play it safe," Churiello whispered over his shoulder. Then he stood up.

"Excuse me, your honor, if it pleases the court, and if the defense has no objection, I would like to suggest that, owing to the lateness of the hour, we recess until Monday morning."

Judge Sterling Williams looked at his watch. "Mr. Coughlin?"

Coughlin looked at Churiello suspiciously. Things weren't going well for his client. He had expected the prosecution to want to wrap things up and send the case to the jury as soon as possible. Now he wondered what the county was trying to pull. He hesitated, but the bottom line was that he was grateful for the unexpected delay.

"The defense has no objection, your honor."

"That being the case, this court stands in recess until ten o'clock Monday morning."

Dugan heard the judge's gavel crack behind him as he quickly pushed through the courtroom doors. He decided to drive the three-quarters of a mile to the District Forest Service Office rather than call from his own. They would have better maps if he needed them. As he hurriedly pushed into the office, he was greeted with a nod from the receptionist and directed to the radio in the district supervisor's office.

"We've got an open channel to Clay Butte," Mattie told him. "Hank, you still there? I've got Sheriff Dugan here."

"Mick, can you hear me?"

"Loud and clear, Hank. What's up?"

"The Barstow kids got separated from their parents up north of Park Rapids. Craig is still out there looking for them. Carolyn's on her way here. In fact, I can see Rick's chopper now. I've got some people on horseback covering the trails. I thought maybe you could bring your dogs up and we could try tracking them."

"No problem, Hank. What's the situation up there?"

"We've got several good sized fires north of Granite Lake, but the teams have them pretty well contained and they're moving in the right direction. But you never know. I want those kids and their dad out of there before nightfall."

"Don't blame you there. What about logistics?"

"Your man's back at Cody, but I think he had some sort of mechanical problem. Rick's got to refuel, but maybe he can fly you back if the winds stay down. You copy, Rick?"

"Can do."

Dugan winced. He had flown with Littlejohn before.

"Is Macauley up there?" the sheriff asked.

"Haven't seen him since lunchtime, you, Richie?" Volas shook his head.

"I'll track him down and send him up. If you see him before I talk to him, just have him stay there. Guy knows the area pretty well. He might be able to help."

"How soon will you be ready, Sheriff?" Littlejohn inquired, breaking in.

Dugan lived south of town, along the Shoshone River.

"I'll be at my house in less than half an hour. Better give me another fifteen to twenty minutes to get my dogs and gear together. You want to pick me up there or have me meet you at the airport?"

"Either way. About six to one, half-a-dozen to the other."

"How about I meet you at the airport at five?"

"Sounds good."

"I'm on my way."


Rick Littlejohn placed his helicopter on the graded parking area ten yards south of the tower at Clay Butte. He reached across Dr. Barstow and helped her unlatch her door. Under other circumstances that could have been fun.

Carolyn Barstow climbed out of the aircraft. She instinctively crouched to avoid the churning rotor. Her legs were a little wobbly. Lactic acid had built up in her muscles following her forced march. She was met by Hank Thurston, who embraced her, as Littlejohn lifted off and headed for Cody. Thurston held his friend for a moment. He was going to tell her not to worry. Then he thought the better of it.

"We've got to get people up there, Hank."

"I've got Mick Dugan coming up with a team of dogs. They're first rate. We'll find them."

"Can't we get anybody up there sooner?"

"I've got one of my rangers and Jill Curtis covering the trails on horseback. Another team is heading up from Beartooth Lake. We've still got a couple of spotter planes in the air, and the fire crews have been notified. Somebody will come across them." Thurston hoped she wouldn't ask him to send anybody else in. At this time of day he wanted people out, not in.

"How serious are the fires?"

"Well, at this time of year, and being as dry as it's been, any fire is serious. But you heard the spotters. The crews have things under control, and the fires are moving in the right direction."

That assumed that the teenagers weren't moving in the wrong direction.

"I can't believe this is happening. Things were going so well. We caught up with Sophie Wednesday and tagged her and her cubs yesterday. All we had to do today was take a nice leisurely hike home. And now this. It's like a bad dream."

"Try not to worry," Thurston told her after all. It sounded just as hollow as he had expected it would, but what the hell, he had to tell her something.

"Yaponcha, here is some pahos," Gogyeng Sowhuti offers the wind god. "Must you help Masauwu test the Son of Light?"

"Masauwu is right. His spirit must be tested. You must not interfere."

Gogyeng Sowuhti called upon the Kachinas to dance. When the Kachinas danced there was rain.

The Shoshone People sent one of their own to meet the Son of Light. He would be the Pahana's guide.

*Western wildfires turn aggressive in the afternoon as temperatures rise and the humidity drops off, but that wasn't the only problem on this day. On this day a cold front moved in from the north and breathed new life into the flames. New life and new direction. Ridges were scaled and surmounted, lines were breached, safety zones were jeopardized. Then the front from the north collided with the usual afternoon warm air over Yellowstone Lake. Enormous dark cumulus clouds rose over the great western lake, precipitating swirling winds, thunder and lightning. In some places there was rain.*

# Chapter Eighteen

Dugan noticed the change as soon as he stepped outside. The temperature had dropped by at least ten degrees and the sky was darkly overcast. It was the area's usual late afternoon cloud over.

Almost every day, when the sun receded just enough, large, dark cumulus clouds would form west of the divide and build over Lake Yellowstone. They would rise high into the sky, promise the area relief from the heat and the drought, flash a few bolts of lightning, rumble with thunder and then move on to taunt the next county and Montana. This time it was different. This time there was wind.

Dugan headed east, back into town, before tuning south on 291 towards Cedar Mountain and the Buffalo Bill Reservoir. The large digital clock/temperature readout at the Cody Savings and Loan told him that the temperature had dropped to 87 degrees, the lowest afternoon temperature the region had seen in a month. Low humidity combined with the drop from the high ninety degree temperature to make the rushing air outside the sheriff's Chevy Blazer almost feel cool. For one moment Mick Dugan actually thought about rolling up the driver's side window of his vehicle. Then he laughed.

Just south of the cutoff that circled the south bank of the reservoir and led back to route 20, raindrops began to splatter Dugan's windshield. The raindrops were large, heavy and occasional. They sporadically pelted the hood and roof with a metallic *splunk*, and they marked the glass with a flat, dirty splat. Dugan had seen it all summer long – a brief, localized cloud burst that would kick up dust, maybe even make the road slick for a few minutes, and then move on. Even so, Dugan couldn't help but enjoy the rich, astringent aroma of freshly wetted mountain pine trees and the sweet smell of dusty hayfields as he drove along the Shoshone River. When he turned up the still dusty dirt road that paralleled the stream by his home, Mick Dugan automatically said a little prayer of thanks.

The sheriff wasted little time once he got home. Four sundry dogs dug themselves out of the various refuges from the heat they had fashioned beneath outbuildings and equipment to come greet him. Two were Labs, one black, one yellow; one was a Golden. The fourth dog was an unusual mix of Airedale and Border Collie that Dugan had spotted at the local pound. The dogs barked, spun, and wrestled with each other in joyful excitement. For the moment, he ignored them. Dugan gathered his tracking harnesses and lines from their pegs in the barn and placed them in the back of his truck. The sight of the working equipment sent the dogs into a frenzy of anticipation.

Dugan trotted to his house where he was met on the porch by his wife.

"What's all the excitement?"

"Couple of lost kids up near the border."

Mrs. Dugan nodded gravely, but she was relieved. At least it wasn't a manhunt.

Dugan filled a two-quart canteen from the kitchen tap and slung it over his shoulder. He picked up a small backpack containing a space blanket, matches, a hand held lantern, wool shirt, light jacket, rain gear, gloves and an extra coil of rope and batteries. He discarded the rain gear, knowing he would be happy to be soaking wet where he was going. His hand ax and hunting knife were kept in the Blazer.

"You seen my hard hat?"

It was supposed to be with his gear, but it was the one piece of equipment he could not get his kids not to play with.

"Look in Jeremy's room."

"I've told that boy..."

"He just wants to be like his dad."

Dugan found the yellow plastic hard hat on his son's dresser. He checked the batteries in the lamp he had strapped to the front, making the hat into a miner's helmet. Dugan put fresh batteries into the light and dropped a few spares into his pocket. He was ready to roll.

"Here, take this," his wife commanded. She held out a sack dinner weighing two pounds. "And make sure you eat it."

Dugan reached out to take the lunch. Instead, he grabbed his wife's wrist and pulled her towards him, holding her close for a moment.

"You be careful now, you hear?"

Dugan kissed her and let her go.

"I will."

He picked up his gear and his lunch and walked quickly to his vehicle which by this time was encircled by four spinning, fidgeting, whining and barking dogs, each hoping to be chosen. Dugan opened the back of his Blazer and made his decision.

"Jackson, Ricki: Kennel!"

Jackson was the big black Lab. He had the nose of a Bloodhound and the heart and desire of a racehorse. Ricki was the strange mix of Border Collie and Airedale. She had wirery black and brown hair, a slightly truncated snout, ears that half stood up and half flopped over, intelligence that was near human, and intuition that was uncanny.

The chosen two leapt into the Blazer with glee. The two remaining dogs whined and barked and spun more than ever, hoping by their enthusiasm to overturn the results of the election, but it was too late. The judgment had been made and was final. Mick Dugan slammed up the tailgate and closed the lift-glass. He climbed into the front seat and drove down the drive. It was only then that he noticed that it was still raining.

*Good deal.*

Guy Macauley also could not help but notice it was raining as he wound his way back northwest along the Chief Joseph Highway. His four-wheel-drive jeep was made for slow, off road use, not high speed, or even normal speed, hairpin turns, especially on wet surfaces. On top of that, he was getting wet, having not bothered to put up the canvass and plastic top. Just past Crandall Ranger Station, Macauley's radio squawked, but the call was broken with static from the mountains and the electrical storm. The message was garbled. He decided to stop in once again at the Clarks Fork general store and check in with the office.

"Mind if I use your phone, Hallie?"

"Local call?" the wizened old storekeeper checked.

"Cody."

"Help yourself."

Macauley stepped behind the counter and dialed the older style rotary phone.

"Marcie? – Guy. You trying to raise me a few minutes ago?"

"I sure enough was, Guy. Where are you now?"

"Clarks Fork"

"Good. Mick wants you to go back up to Clay Butte and wait for him there."

"Something wrong?"

"Something about lost kids. I'm not sure. Mick was in a hurry. He just wanted to be sure you'd meet him there if you could."

"Mick bringing dogs?"

"I expect he is."

"He driving up?"

"Rick Littlejohn's flying him up."

Macauley looked out the window. It was still raining and now blowing to beat the band. He was going to have one wet ass before he was through.

"It's raining pretty good up here. Wind's kicking around pretty good too. What's it doing in Cody?"

"It's raining here too."

Macauley wasn't so certain Littlejohn would be able to ferry Dugan up if current conditions held.

"Tell Mick I'll be there.

"Thanks," he told the storekeeper.

"'S all right," she let him know, not bothering to look up from her newspaper.

Macauley knew what was expected. He picked out a small bottle of grape juice from the refrigerator case and a twist of elk jerky from the jar near the register. He lay two dollars on the counter and did not wait for change.

Outside it was pouring rain. The deputy sheriff had no choice but to raise the canvass top now, something he should have done a half-hour ago. He looked out across the vista. The sky was dark and heavy to the south and northeast. It seemed lighter due north and northwest. Guy Macauley wondered if it was raining north of 212, the Beartooth Highway.

*Sure hope so.*

Hank Thurston looked out the large screened windows to the south. He saw the dark clouds over the Sunlight Basin and the Wapiti Valley. He prayed they would keep coming north. At 4:33 p.m. there was no rain in the Beartooth Mountains or the Absaroka Wilderness. There was, however, wind. Enough wind so that Thurston and Volas had to close most of the windows in the tower to keep maps and papers from blowing off the table and the desk. Thick cumulus clouds rose high into the sky. The clouds were dark, but so far no rain had fallen. There was also thunder.

"Richie, I want you to run Mrs. Barstow down to Hunter Peak."

"Now hold on a minute, Hank," Carolyn Barstow protested. "I'm staying right here. And I'm going out with that search party you're organizing."

"It's better if you go back to the ranch. Really. Look, I know you're worried, and I'm sure you're pumped up with adrenaline right now, but you've got to be exhausted. And when was the last time you had anything to eat? All we've got here are Twinkies."

"They'll do. Besides, I'm not hungry."

"I know you're not. And I know that you can hike most of my rangers to hell and gone. But the fact of the matter is that at some point exhaustion is going to set in, and when it does, you'll be a hindrance not a help."

Dr. Carolyn Barstow knew Thurston was right. Still, the thought of being back at the guest ranch, where she would have no idea what the situation was, was unacceptable.

"How about if I just stay here? I won't go out with you, and I won't interfere."

"Really, Carolyn, I think it's best if you go back to the ranch."

"It's okay, Hank. I know you'll have to call your people in soon. You do what you have to do. I just want to stay here."

Thurston wasn't happy, but if she could do it so could he.

"Richie, run down to Hunter Peak and ask Sandy if she can spare any leftovers. Tell her to put 'em on the Barstow's bill."

Carolyn Barstow almost smiled.

The rain bouncing off the curved, corrugated sheet metal roof of the hangar housing Spirit Mountain Aviation made such a racket that the people seeking shelter inside had to shout to be heard.

"I don't suppose you can fly in this?" Sheriff Dugan asked Rick Littlejohn.

"Not a chance. Even if the rain lets off, there's too much wind shear and gust spread."

"Any idea how long this is supposed to last?"

"Hard to say. Weather service says we're on the edge of two fronts. High pressure from the north, low from the southwest."

"They getting rain in the Absaroka?"

"Not last time we checked, about ten minutes ago."

"Damn. Can you raise Hank Thurston?"

"We can try."

The two men walked across the hangar floor to the office in the rear corner.

"Rita, the sheriff wants to talk to Hank."

"Hey, handsome. Anything for you."

The woman played with some knobs on the radio to her left. There was static from the storm, but she was able to make contact.

"Hey, Hank, got some competition for you here. Just my luck, he wants to talk to you."

Dugan took the mike.

"Hank, it's Mick. We got us a nice little storm here, how about you?"

"We can see the storm, Mick, but so far all we have is wind. This keeps up and we'll likely see a blowup. I'm pulling everybody out except the fire crews. That'll be their call. How soon can you get here."

"That's a good question. We can't fly in this. You want me to wait it out, or should I drive on up?"

"Any idea how long the storm is expected to last?"

"Hard to say. Even if the rain lets up, I don't think Rick can fly in this wind."

Littlejohn confirmed that opinion with a shake of his head.

"Then you better drive on up, Mick. We got to find those kids soon."

"On my way. Is Macauley there yet?"

"He just got here, soaked to the bone. You want to talk to him."

"Yeah, I'm afraid I do."

"You hear that, Guy?"

"Got it. What's up, Mick?"

"Guy, I'm sorry about this, but I may need you to come back to Cody. Wait at the airport with Littlejohn."

Macauley thought *damn*, but said, "You're the boss, Mick. What's up?"

"I'm going to try and get another dog team in for backup. I want you here to meet him if Rick still can't fly him up. If Rick can fly by the time he gets here, you can fly back with them."

"On my way. Mitch got a spare set of clothes? I'm soaked to the bone."

"I'll ask. Tell Hank I'm heading out now."

"Get here as fast as you can, Mick, but don't kill yourself on the way," Thurston called over.

"Do my best."

Before Mick Dugan left the Spirit Mountain hangar he made a phone call.

*The Kachinas danced but it was not enough. Their magic was not strong enough against the magic of the Great Plumed Serpent and Yaponcha and Masauwu the Skeleton Man.*

*There was no rain in the Shoshone near Lost Lake, three miles south-west of the fires. There was no rain in the Absaroka near Granite Lake and Thiel Lake and Burnt Bacon. There was no rain north of the 212. There was only lightning and wind. And now new fires.*

# Chapter Nineteen

"Jess, that Burnt Bacon fire looks to be crowning. Same thing for the one by Thiel," the spotter in the C-47 reported from five thousand feet above the mountains.

"What direction they moving, Russ?"

"Hard to say. Winds got things riled up pretty good, but it looks like they're still moving northeast 'bout a half-mile an hour. Uh oh. Looks like we got a new one southwest of Granite, between Granite and Lost Lake, and another one due south of Lower Granite. Must've come from the afternoon lightning."

"How's that one look?"

"It hasn't crowned yet, but it's speadin' pretty good. Looks like eight to ten acres burnin' there, maybe more and really running."

"Heading for Granite Lake?"

"Petty much."

"How's the Native Lake fire look," Fred Jenkins of the Red Lodge team asked."

"Not too bad, Fred. You got a line maybe fifteen hundred yards long and a hundred yards wide almost due north moving up the east side of the gulch. Should take care of itself once it reaches the ridge."

"You copy all that, Clay Butte?"

"We got it Jess," Hank Thurston confirmed. Arthur Marshall was busy on another frequency calling in a team from Prescott National Forest.

"Jill, Matthew, are you listening?" Thurston called.

"We're 'ere, 'ank," Matthew Hunter reported as best he could. The topography, atmospherics, and electrical storm were playing havoc with his hand held set, not to mention dying batteries. "We're at the 'ampsite... No sign of anybod...."

"I want you both out. All other teams are already out or getting out. I want you two out now. Copy?"

" 'opy. On our way."

"Keep your eyes peeled, but don't waste any time. I want you out before nightfall."

" 'opy."

---

"We were on the top of the world, Jon, at least I was. Hah! There's a good one for you. That's what they call the area around Beartooth Pass. Anyway, back then I thought we had it made. Business boom-ing, farm in order, dogs and horses and working on a kid. I had it knocked. Then I screwed up."

"That's bullshit."

"Maybe, maybe not. You know, it had been such a great sum-mer, around here leastwise, and things were going so well I knocked off early that day, figuring on taking care of chores and getting in a swim. But I knew something was wrong as soon as I got out of the truck..."

"So that was how Sheriff Dugan got your husband involved," Andersen surmised.

"Exactly. It was a beautiful summer evening. Joshua was putting in long hours, trying to get as much done as possible, but he came home a little early that day, and I was just starting to put togeth-er some supper when the telephone rang. It was a phone call that changed our lives."

"I remember it like it was yesterday, Jon.

"I had knocked off early, so it was only about six-thirty when I got home. I parked over by the barn, figuring to change my boots and get right to the chores. I knew Kris knew I was home because the row the dogs made was a dead give-away every time. I expected her to come out and give me a hug first chance she had, like she usually did, but when I saw her charge out the door shouting at me, I knew something was wrong."

"*Josh! Pick up the phone! – It's an emergency!*"

"I ran to the phone in the barn and took the receiver off the wall. It was Mick Dugan, the sheriff out in Park County, Wyoming, and he had a real problem on his hands."

"Mr. Travis, this is Mick Dugan out in Cody, Wyoming. I don't know if you remember me, sir, but I met you last year out at that seminar you put on at Colter Bay Lodge."

"I remember you, Sheriff. Goldens, Labs, and Border Collies… and one mutt."

"Yes sir, that's right. Well, we got a bit of a situation out here, and I thought I'd touch base with you."

"What's up, Sheriff?"

"We got two teenagers lost up near the state line in the Beartooth Mountains. Their dad is out looking for them, but we don't know exactly where he is either. I wouldn't be botherin' you except that we got some fires in the area. I was just wondering if you had any advice or suggestions."

"How close are the fires?"

"Hard to say 'cause we don't know where the people are."

"How big are they?"

"Big enough, hundred and forty to a hundred and sixty acres apiece, last I heard, but that may have changed. It's been dryer than Hades out here all summer, and now the wind's kicking up. We've actually got rain here in Cody, but I checked with the ranger, and the rain hasn't hit up there yet. Don't know if it will."

"Well, I don't know what to tell you, Sheriff. Don't worry about doing anything wrong. Just go with your best dogs and your gut feeling. Your guess is as good as mine, probably better. One thing, Mick, ah, I don't know exactly how to say this, but if things are as rough as you say out there, what with the rugged terrain and the fire and all, you might have to think about cutting your losses. Send too many searchers out and you may lose as many as you find, especially at night."

"That's why I'm going in alone. It's already becoming a three-ring circus up there. Thurston's had all kinds of people out looking the better part of the day. He's the supervising ranger. Any chance you and those dogs of yours could get out here, real quick like? The fire's liable to spread fast and I could sure use the backup. I know I'm askin' a lot, and I wouldn't normally ask a civilian, Mr. Travis, but, the truth be known, none of us was out at Jenny Lake consider you a civilian."

Joshua accepted the compliment even though he knew it would cost him his weekend and maybe a whole lot more.

"I'll see what I can work out. The sheriff here might be able to pull some strings with the air guard. Give me a number that can patch me through to you in the field. If you need me, or if you find the kids, call the Lincoln County Sheriff's Office."

———— ∿∿ ————

"I gave him your number, Jon, and then just told him, *Good luck.*"

"I remember. We tried to get the jets from Wausau Paper and Wausau Insurance, but they were all tied up. And we had talked about the possibility of using the military to transport you and the dogs to search sites, but that was the first time we actually tried it."

"Good thing you had already done some leg work. You being a full colonel and Korean War hero to boot went a long way."

*Not long enough*, VanStavern knew.

**Harrison:** So it was you, Sheriff Dugan, who asked Mr. Travis to participate in the search?

**Dugan:** Yes, sir.

**Harrison:** Why did you feel it was necessary or desirable to involve a civilian?

**Dugan:** I had met Mr. Travis at a tracking seminar he conducted at Colter Bay Lodge, and I had seen Mr. Travis and his dogs work. My dogs are good but I've never seen another team that could hold a candle to Mr. Travis and his dogs.

**Carton:** Just how did you intend to get him here from Wisconsin, on the wings of eagles?

**Dugan:** Mr. Travis said he would take care of those logistics. That was good enough for me. Turned out he got here in three hours and change.

**Harrison:** How did you plan on getting him from Cody to the search site.

**Dugan:** Rick Littlejohn was to fly him in if possible. I also sent Guy Macauley back to Cody in order to drive him up if it wasn't

possible to fly. Guy was to act as his
    guide to the actual search site once they
    got up to Clay Butte or closer.
**Baxter:** So it was your decision that paired
    up Guy Macauley with Joshua Travis.
**Dugan:** Yes, sir, I guess it was.

*Joshua Travis decides to take Jenny-Dog and a dog named Ellie. Ellie
is a Golden Retriever/Labrador cross that some neighbor kids had found
a few years back when she was just a pup. Some fool had dropped her off
to fend for herself, at the ripe old age of eight weeks, alongside the road
where the kids were riding their bikes. They wanted to keep her, of course,
but they already had two dogs and their mom said no and made them take
her over to Joshua. Everyone in Lincoln County knew that Joshua rarely
said no to dogs or kids.*

*And Ellie turned out just dandy. She loves to hunt and she loves to
play and she loves all people, especially kids. She is about the willingest
worker you could ever hope to have, but Joshua's only been working her
seriously for a little over a year. Jenny-Dog is in a class by herself, but
Ellie is a close second. She rolls her upper lip in a grin when Joshua calls
her, and she wriggles all over the place when he pats her. But when he asks
her to work she is right there.*

*Travis grabs lines and harnesses out of the tack room and has the dogs
wait on the porch while he gets his duffel and his pack. He goes over things
in his mind, waiting for VanStavern to drive him down to Wausau. He
considers the equipment he will need and how to best handle things, but
he knows that until he sees the situation on the ground he is just guessing.
He has lights and compasses, knives and a good hand ax and field shovel.
He has a down bag and a solar tarp, and he has packed a first-aid kit and
extra canteens. He throws in a hard hat and an extra coil of rope, but he
can't let himself be too weighted down, especially at night.*

*Joshua puts most of the gear in the duffel, keeping the pack as light as possible. Then Kristian comes over, hands him his freshly packed lunch bucket and takes his arm.*

*"It sounds like a rough one."*

*Joshua nods in agreement.*

*"Do you want me to come with you?" she asks, afraid of the answer whatever it might be.*

*Joshua looks deep into his wife's beautiful green eyes thinking, God, yes I want you to come with me. I want you on the plane and on the ground and to hug my arm, like you're doing now, and to cheer me on with your glances and your smile.*

*"No. You'd best stay here."*

*Where the hell is Jonathan, he wonders. Let's get this show on the road. And he feels like he did back in high school on the night of a big game when everything was against his team and everything was riding on him.*

*They hear the siren on VanStavern's squad car coming and he looks up. He has a bad feeling deep in his gut, but he doesn't say anything. He hugs his wife and holds onto her longer than he means to. He throws his pack onto his right shoulder and picks up his duffel and tracking gear with his other hand. He whistles to the dogs and sends them out to meet the patrol car coming up the drive.*

---

"I had never seen Joshua like he was when he left for that rescue in Cody, and it frightened me," Kristian explained. "He was calm, as always, but he seemed aloof and fidgety. I knew he was anxious to get going, but when the sheriff's car finally came and he hugged me, he held me longer than I thought he would. And when he held me at arms-length and looked into my eyes, just before turning to go to the car, I saw something that scared the heck out of me."

"What was that, Kris?"

"Part of it was the memory of my father, the last time I saw him, just before he walked out... But more than that was the realization that Joshua, himself, was scared. And that was something I had never seen before."

"Really?"

"Now that I look back, I don't know how I could have ever missed it."

"You know, Jon, I'm always nervous en route to a rescue, but it's usually a tight-wound, excited nervousness like I used to feel waiting for the opening kickoff at a Friday night game. But that time I had a sinking feeling in my gut and a worry somewhere deep in my chest that I just couldn't get a handle on. And I gotta tell you, Jon, when we drove to Wausau and I saw that the only plane waiting for us was a C-130 prop job, I was so pissed off that I didn't know whether to curse or to cry."

"The runway was too short for a big jet. The Hercules was all we could come up with on such short notice."

Joshua nodded. "I knew that outfit would take a good two or three hours to get into Cody, and I figured on at least another hour or two to get to the search site. Actually, it turned out to be closer to three. The kids had been missing since morning, and it was 7:30 in the evening, Wisconsin time. Dugan had said the winds were strong and erratic, and that not only were they moving the fires along quickly, but they were also playing havoc with the fire lines. I knew it was going to be one helluva search."

*As the fat, noisy airplane lumbers into the sky, he prays that the kids will turn up before he gets there. The simple truth is that despite all his confidence in his dogs, and all their past successes, he knows too much is working against them this time.*

"I just didn't think I would find those kids that night."

"My God, Kris, did he?"
Kristian looked at the writer and frowned. "Yes."

*Skeleton Man and the Great Plumed Serpent and Yaponcha worked their magic. Together, they opened the doors to Topqolu, Hell.*

*The fires continued to grow exponentially, cheered on by the strong and gusting winds. Entire mountainsides were now ablaze. Dark billowing smoke and towering orange flames, hundreds of feet in height, were clearly visible. From Clay Butte the fires appeared as glowing lights or coals from a summer cookout. From ground zero they were rapidly becoming the Gates of Hell.*

# Chapter Twenty

Dugan drove his Blazer to the Marathon gas pump and filled both his tanks. He flicked on his siren and the flashing lights on his light bar as he sped into town and turned north on 120 as fast as he dared on the rain slick roads. The dogs braced themselves and whined in the back. Mick Dugan drove the same Scenic Highway that Guy Macauley had driven an hour earlier. His Blazer was wider and longer than Macauley's jeep, but it was still no match for the hairpin curves and switchbacks of the Chief Joseph. His siren was blaring and his lights were flashing, cutting through the blinding rain, but Dugan still had to drive carefully or he would inevitably run himself, or someone else, off the side of one of the mountains. Dugan floored it on the long straight grades, both up and down. He braked gently into the curves and accelerated coming out. Driving like a mad man, he managed to average forty-five miles per hour. That made it just after seven p.m. when he arrived at Clay Butte. The air was cooler than it had been in Cody, but it wasn't raining. He was surprised that he hadn't passed Macauley coming the other way. *Must have missed him in the rain* was what he figured. That rain had ended before he reached Crandall Station and then Clay Butte.

Hank Thurston climbed down from the tower to meet Dugan. Thurston had a map rolled up under his arm. Arthur Marshall barked orders to the fire crews via the radio. Carolyn Barstow sat at a picnic table on the edge of the parking area, terribly mesmerized by the smoke in the distance.

"Howdy, Mick. Thanks for coming."

"Hell of a downpour in Cody."

They walked over to the woman who was fondling but not drinking a cold cup of coffee.

"Carolyn, you remember Sheriff Dugan."

"Yes, of course, Sheriff. Please find my children."

"We'll sure try, ma'am."

"Carolyn, show Mick exactly where you made camp just like you showed me."

Thurston spread the topographical map across the picnic table. He and Dugan held down the corners to keep it from blowing in the wind.

"It was right here, Sheriff, north of Park Rapids, just north of the border. This is the main trail here. We followed a deer path here to the left of this dried out pond and meadow. Over here is where Gretchen and Carl went to pick berries this morning," She explained, pointing to small open areas to the east. "It can't be much more than a half a mile from our campsite."

Dugan looked at the woman. She was holding together pretty well, all things considered, but Dugan knew it was taking remarkable effort.

"The smokejumpers have widened this stretch of the stream bed," Thurston told Dugan, showing him an area south and east of the campsite. "Between you and me, I'm going to ask Arthur to have them try to push the line a little north if they can. We got fires here, here, here, and now we got one here," Thurston explained, pointing to the locations on the map. The new fires, started by the afternoon thunderstorm, were located south and southwest of Granite Lake. "The Red Lodge and Missoula teams have cut a break here, west of Native Lake. Art Marshall found us another team out of Prescott,

Arizona, and he's got some flatlanders coming in from Minnesota. The Prescott crew is working in this area here, trying to cut a break between these two lakes."

"That Lost Lake?"

"Yup. This one up here is Lake Reno ."

"Right. Which way are the fires moving?"

"North-northeast, more or less, towards Granite, but these up here are jumping all over the place." Thurston indicated the areas near Burnt Bacon and Thiel lakes.

"Kids know enough to make for safe areas, lakes or bogs and whatnot?"

"Yes, they do," Dr. Barstow answered. "If there's enough light."

"What's the best way in, Hank?"

"Best way's to two-track it down Muddy Creek and push as far past the lower lake fork as we can. We'll have to hoof it from there."

"We?"

"We."

Dugan nodded.

"Let's go."

Thurston took Carolyn Barstow's hand in his.

"I still think you ought to go back to Sandy's."

"I'll be all right. And thank you. Thank you both."

"We'll do our best," Dugan told her, then he remembered, "Dang, I almost forgot, I got another dog team coming in."

"Say again?"

"I got a team coming in from Wisconsin for backup. Best damn dog handler you ever saw. I got Macauley and Littlejohn waiting for him at Cody. One or the other'll get them here, depending on weather."

"I'll show them where we camped and how to get in," Mrs. Barstow volunteered.

"Richie can show them the map."

"And Macauley knows this area like the back of his hand."

"I'll show them."

Dugan was somewhat familiar with the area and the terrain. He had even used the same area himself once or twice during hunting season. It would take three or more hours to get there, so long as the Blazer didn't get hung up. And so long as it didn't get too dark too quick.

"Where's Mr. Barstow?" Dugan asked.

"He stayed at the camp, in case the children came back," Dr. Barstow replied.

That was good thinking, and for the first time Dugan began to feel that things might not be too bad after all. Hell, if it hadn't been for the damn fires, he would have been downright confident.

Inside the Blazer, away from Carolyn Barstow, Dugan asked, "How fast are the fires moving?"

"Half-mile to a mile an hour, where they've crowned, and they're jumping. We got a running crown fire in this area here and here, and we got spot ground fires to the southwest and northeast. The ground fires are running a lot faster and in this wind they'll crown soon, if they haven't already. Ground cover's like paper and the trees are so dry that everything's going up."

"*Great.*"

Mrs. Barstow still wanted to come along, despite being exhausted, but Sheriff Dugan convinced her it would be better for her to stay behind and wait for Mr. Travis and his deputy. He tried not to sound worried, but the truth was he sure wished that the man and those dogs he had seen work out at Jenny Lake were with him now. They left Richie Volas, who was closing in on twenty-four straight duty hours, with Mrs. Barstow after making damn sure he understood where the campsite was. Volas was a good man, but this was his first fire and it would be no easy task finding that camp after dark, even for Macauley. And by the time Joshua Travis got there it would be dark. Damn dark.

"Guy, you're dripping wet. Don't you go sitting on the good furniture now, hear? You home for good?"

"Just to get changed…"

"Daddy got wet! Daddy got wet!" Annie taunted in a singsong voice.

"C'mere, Pumpkin. Want a hug?"

"Noooo! You're all wet!"

"Hank find those teenagers?" Mrs. Macauley asked.

"Not yet. Mick's got his dogs. Should be up there now."

"How bad are the fires?"

"Don't know for sure. Could be bad with the year we been having. That storm this afternoon started another fire south of Granite Lake. Wouldn't want my kids running around up there."

Billy Macauley kicked off his boots in the mud room.

"Evening, sir. I got the chores all done."

His son had recently taken to addressing him as 'sir' for some reason. Macauley didn't demand it, but he didn't discourage it either.

"Evening, son. You clean Cisco's hooves?"

"Yes, sir, and I helped Annie do Jasper. Only thing I didn't do was brush Jimmy 'cause he was too wet."

Macauley nodded to his son. "I thank you son. I'm glad I can count on you."

Guy Macauley went into the bedroom and put on a clean, dry, freshly ironed uniform.

"Where you off to now, Guy?" his wife inquired.

"Heading into Cody. Mick's got another dog team coming in. My guess is it's this guy he met in the Teton's last year. I'm going to meet him and get him up to Clay Butte one way or another."

"Can't you stay for dinner?"

"I'd best be heading out. I'll grab something fast in town."

"I'll hug you now, daddy," Annie offered.

"Why you're just a fair weather friend, ain't you?"

Annie nodded unabashedly, having no idea what that meant. Macauley scooped her up in his arms, then he kissed his wife. He put his daughter back on the floor and headed out to the porch.

"Son, can I see you a moment."

"Yes, sir," Billy acknowledged, just a little concerned.

Once out on the porch Guy Macauley told him, "Son, I don't know when I might be getting back. I may need you take care of the chores tomorrow morning. Think you can handle it? I don't want to trouble your momma."

Billy Macauley was shaking with excitement. The morning chores were a lot of work and a lot of responsibility, especially for one man or, as in this case, one ten-year-old boy. "Yes, sir."

"The keys to the Power Wagon are under the seat. Take your time and be careful. Understand?"

"Yes, sir." Billy Macauley was grinning from ear to ear, bursting with pride.

Guy Macauley wasn't grinning, but he too was bursting with pride.

*Gogyeng Sowuhti was exhausted. None of her magic was working. Her heart was glad to see the Shoshone guide team up with the Son of Light. He would help.*

*By dusk the fires were out of control. Fanned by high winds, the Lost Lake fire raced through parched meadows and dry forests faster than many an experienced hand would have believed possible. By nightfall it had crowned and encompassed more than one thousand acres. The fires in the north had also crowned. Tremendous flames roiled across the forest canopy using heat and vacuum, temperature inversion and convection to create their own weather. Sectors expected to burn for days were devoured in hours. And there were blowups.*

# Chapter Twenty-one

*At Cronin's, in San Francisco, things have quieted down. It is too late in the evening for the dinner crowd and too early in the week for an after-theatre crowd. The rain has settled into a steady, dreary downpour.*

"After Joshua left, I took care of the chores. I had supper almost prepared but I couldn't eat.

"I told myself I was being foolish and not to read things into the matter that weren't really there. I wasn't about to let myself get all bent out of shape like I almost did after that first rescue."

*And perhaps like you did a little this last time?* Andersen wondered.

"I had gotten much better about watching Joshua go off on a search. He had gone on many by then, and he always came back safe and sound and usually in pretty good spirits. Still, I found it best to have some company nearby for some of the rescues he went out on, especially the ones that seemed to present danger to Joshua himself.

"I would have called my friend Maggie, but she was in Chicago looking for work. The Green family, some good friends of ours, was off gallivanting around somewhere during summer vacation as usual. I could have gone over to the farm and spent time with Josh's family, or gone to the VanStaverns' since Jon would be the most in touch with the situation. Instead, I decided to just stay where I was and tough it out. Hell, I was a big girl, wasn't I?"

"Uh oh."

"Exactly. I tried to keep busy with work, or reading, or even just straightening up the house. Anything to keep my mind occupied, but it was no use. I really did need some company after all, so finally I broke down and let Jesse, our Border Collie, well Border Collie-something mix, probably Australian Shepherd, into the house. Then I called Jane."

"Uh oh again."

*"Hey, kiddo, what's up? God, Kris, you and Joshua have to get out here and see my new place. Wait, wait, listen." Jane held the receiver towards the open window facing the beach. "Can you hear it?"*

*"Sounds wonderful, Jane. How are you doing?"*

*Jane knew Kristian too well. There was something in her voice. She hesitated before telling her friend, "All right, let's have it. Where's he off to this time?"*

*"Wyoming."*

*"So, what's the problem? Hell, you guys are always talking about how damn beautiful the mountains are, and you were just out there last year. You said Josh loves it out there. How come he didn't take you?"*

*"There's a fire."*

*"A fire? You mean like a forest fire?"*

*"Yes."*

*"Is it a big one. I read somewhere that most forest fires are only a few acres. How big is this one?"*

*"I don't know."*

*"Oh, hell, I wouldn't worry. Josh is a big boy. He can take care of himself. Did you ever take out that humungous insurance policy on him like I told you?"*

*Kristian smiled. She hadn't.*

*"Jesus, Kris, I told you, the first time you marry for money. The second time you can marry for love. Hey, speaking of which, you'll never guess who I ran into the other day."*

*"Who?"*

*"Kenny!"*

*"Kenny-Kenny?"*

*"Yep, Kenny-Kenny. We're getting together tomorrow night."*

*"He's not married?"*

*"Didn't take. How could it, it wasn't me."*

*"Well I'll be damned. Be sure and give him my love, will you. But Christ, Jane, take it easy on the poor guy."*

*"Are you kidding, I'm going to burn him down...oops, sorry. Bad choice of words."*

"She actually said that?"

Kristian laughed. It was funny now.

"What did you do?"

"I curled up with Jesse and a cup of coffee in front of the television, watching the ten o'clock news...."

"That damn "hippo" seemed to lumber on forever," Joshua tells his friend, referring to the Hercules cargo plane that flew him and his dogs from Wausau to Cody. "I kept trying to go over things in my mind, but the endless droning of the engines was starting to get to me, and I was getting nauseous. I think it was just after eight o'clock, Rocky Mountain Time, when the pilot called me up to the cockpit and pointed to a reddish-orange glow in the west. It looked real pretty, and at first I thought he was pointing out the sunset. Then it suddenly dawned on me that the horizon was way beyond that glow, and that we were looking at the fires from twenty-five thousand feet up and fifty miles out."

"Must have really been something," VanStavern surmised. Joshua continued.

"My stomach knotted up again. The wind that was buffeting the plane didn't help any. About all I could say was, *shit.*

"Less than twenty minutes later we were on the ground in Cody. They had gotten some rain, but the rain had stopped, and it was windy as hell. It might have still been light, I couldn't tell. The haze from the smoke was blocking out any of what might have been left of the sun. Lights were on like it was midnight, and a deputy sheriff met us at the hatch, waving me towards him with one arm and holding his cowboy hat on with the other."

*"Mr. Travis, I'm Deputy Macauley – Guy Macauley."*

*"How far do we have to go?"*

*"The lookout station is seventy-five miles from here, by car," he tells Joshua as they unload the dogs and his gear, "But we got a chopper waiting if he can get up in these winds."*

*"Good." They run to the waiting helicopter that will ferry them up to the lookout station, and both dogs jump right in. Joshua suspects he smells alcohol on the pilot's breath. Guy Macauley is sure of it. They both hold their tongues.*

*"What do you think, Rick, can we get up?"*

*"Sure, no sweat" Littlejohn answers, and they load the dogs and gear into the chopper.*

*Joshua and Macauley climb in next. Rick Littlejohn takes one last look at the wind sock then takes his place in the pilot's seat muttering to himself.*

*"Not so sure about down."*

"The helicopter ride took longer than I had bargained for but it sure beat driving. The high winds tossed that dang whirlybird around like a badminton birdie. I looked at Macauley without saying a word. We both knew those winds would be a problem on the ground, and a few times I thought we'd be on the ground sooner than we wanted. But that damn chopper pilot knew his stuff, drunk or sober. And by God if he didn't get us all to that ranger outpost in one piece, Jonathan. But it was almost nine p.m., their time, and there was still no sign of the kids."

**Harrison:** Sheriff Dugan, why is it that you and Mr. Thurston didn't take more people with you in the search for the two missing children?

**Dugan:** I knew it would be dark by the time we actually began the search. The winds seemed to be building and there were five fires by then, not just three. It had the makings of a dangerous situation. I didn't even want Hank to come along. He insisted.

**Carton:** How did you plan on evacuating the people once you found them?

**Dugan:** I guess I planned on walking out with them the same way I walked in. I figured it would depend on where I found them. I knew the area up there pretty well, and I had some safety zones in mind, depending on where I linked up with the missing people.

**Carton:** What would you have done if you had come across the campers and one or more of them were down?

**Dugan:** I would have worked with Hank Thurston and the ones who weren't down to evacuate the others.

**Baxter:** What if all of them were down?

**Dugan:** I guess we would have winged it. I would have tried to radio for help, maybe get some help from the fire crews in the

area. To tell you the truth, I figured either we would find the Barstows alive and
well or we wouldn't. I didn't figure there
would be much middle ground.

It was dark by the time Mick Dugan and Hank Thurston made
it to the campsite with Dugan's tracking team. The smell of smoke
rose and fell with the wind. They could also hear the fire. Even at a
distance it reminded Thurston of the World War Two bombers he
had served with, revving up their engines on a British tarmac.

"Fire's spreading fast," Thurston observed.

"Yeah. Let's jury-rig some lights."

Both dogs were off lead, sniffing and peeing, sniffing and peeing.

Thurston searched the campsite with his lantern. The men
found the two high tech, lightweight tents. Inside were sleeping
bags, backpacks with clothing, one sack of dirty clothing and a small
Coleman lantern. A nylon sack was suspended by a rope thrown over
a tree limb twenty-five feet above the ground.

"Must be their food."

"Let's hang a light from there. Maybe give Macauley and Travis
a beacon."

"Good idea, Mick."

The suspended light swayed in the wind. Sections of the site
were illuminated then obscured, depending on which way the lantern swung.

"Where's your friend?" Dugan asked.

"Shit! Craig...! Craig Barstow!" Thurston shouted in different
directions.

"Unless he's just peein' in the woods nearby, he ain't gonna hear
us."

"He must have gone looking for the kids again."

"Hope he found them."

"Yeah. Nothing ever goes easy, does it?"

Now they had three people lost in the woods at night. The fires were spreading rapidly. All in all, things didn't look very promising.

"I'm gonna have the dogs track the kids and hope that Craig is with them."

"Right."

The two men began carefully rummaging through the two tents, guessing in the lantern light just what belonged to whom. The fact that the kids were teenagers made it all the more difficult.

"What about these?" Dugan asked, holding up a pair of Jockey briefs.

"I'd say," Thurston replied, shining his light over them. "Craig's in good shape, but he's no thirty inch waist."

Dugan tossed the briefs to the side.

"How about these moccasins?"

"Hard to say. Let's look for a couple of bras. They should be different sizes."

"Right. We could've used Mrs. Barstow to help sort things out."

Thurston cut him a hard look. Both men searched through the second tent. They located a bag with dirty laundry in it and dumped it out, discovering two bras in the pile. One had fairly small cups and hooked in the front. The other was more substantial with clasps in the back.

"Go with the front loader."

"Right."

"Think that's enough?"

Dugan shined his light around the interior of the tent.

"Look!"

Tucked neatly beneath one of the air pillows were two photographs, one of a young man, the other of the same young man with his arms around Gretchen Barstow.

"Think we can use them for a scent?"

"Don't have to." Dugan handed the pictures to the ranger. "Now we know which sleeping bag is hers. Jack! Ricki! Come!" The two dogs raced to his side.

Sheriff Dugan let his dogs take a scent off the clothes and the sleeping bag and told them to "Find!" He had been training his trackers the way Joshua Travis had shown him a year before in the Tetons, and it always worked pretty slick in practice. Now was the real test.

"Go find!"

*Red Hawk helped as much as he could, but Yaponcha was too strong. He could not fly in the wind and he could not see in the dark. Red Hawk came to ground.*

*The night came on quickly, aided by the black smoke filling the air. The sun and the moon and the stars were all hidden. The only light came from the glow of the fires.*

# Chapter Twenty-two

*"I'll let you out as close to the tower as I can get you," Littlejohn shouts to his passengers. "Hope the lot ain't too full of vehicles."*

*"Your call, Rick," Macauley yells back. "We can run a few yards."*

*"Ain't nothing to call. Ain't no other place. Can't put down on the slope in this wind. Road's too dark and too many trees."*

*"What about Hunter Peak? Sandy can run us up to the tower."*

*"Let's try for the tower. If I can't land there then we'll try something else."*

**Harrison:** Mr. Littlejohn, why did you decide to let your passengers off at Clay Butte rather than the search site?

**Littlejohn:** Too dark, too windy, too many trees, too many mountains, take your pick.

**Harrison:** But couldn't you have gotten them closer than you did?

**Littlejohn:** Off the record?

**Harrison:** Go ahead, Mr Littlejohn, off the record.

**Littlejohn:** (I might have been pushin' the gust differential just a little. My outfit is rated safe for a 15mph differential.

The gusts that night were closer to 25 or 30.)

**Carton:** Mr. Littlejohn, had you been drinking that night?

**Littlejohn:** You want to define drinking.

**Carton:** Had you consumed any alcohol prior to flying that night?

**Littlejohn:** Again, off the record?

**Harrison:** Yes, Mr. Littlejohn.

**Littlejohn:** (You bet your sweet ass I consumed alcohol prior to flying that night. You think I would've flown that night straight?)

**Harrison:** (Might that have influenced your decision not to ferry the Travis search team closer to the search site?)

**Littlejohn:** (Hell yes it influenced my decision, otherwise I would have decided a whole lot sooner.)

*"You must have ice water in your veins, Mr. Littlejohn," Joshua tells the pilot as he off-loads his dogs and gear.*

*"Ain't ice water, sir. Just the right mixture of cheap wine, Bourbon and Dramamine. Sometimes I get it right. You want to have one of those rangers roll some boulders on my runners till I get the blades folded and the runners staked."*

*"Sure thing. Thanks."*

*"Good luck, sir."*

*The Fire People did the best they could, but they were fighting a losing battle. Dog Man and the Dog People did the best they could, but White Wind was not with them, and Dog Man was not the Son of Light.*

*All fires had crowned. Several had linked up. And the fires were running. Running and jumping. Areas once deemed safe were now declared danger zones. No one could tell where the next fire would start or where the fires and gasses would suck the oxygen out of the air.*

# Chapter Twenty-three

Joshua looked out the kitchen window and noticed that it was snowing again. The kitchen was becoming quite warm, but outside the temperature was falling. Joshua needed to reassure himself that he was safe before he continued. "At the lookout station I met a deputy ranger, named Laura something, and the fire supervisor in charge, a guy named Marshall, and a college kid named Richie. I also met Carolyn Barstow, the mother of the lost kids. She was a tall, handsome woman, or would have been under other circumstances, I guess, and she was managing to keep her cool, which must have been harder than heck with all the shouting and running around and smoke and wind and knowing that your kids were lost out there in the dark. She tried to help without getting in the way, and she talked like she knew her way around the woods pretty well."

"Mick said she was a wildlife biologist."

"Something like that. I liked her right off and hoped things would turn out okay. But when Laura showed me the map and told me what the situation was, and the fire supervisor showed me where the fire lines were and how fast they were moving and, to top it all off, handed us gas masks, I wasn't optimistic.

"The terrain was just too rugged and the winds were too high to get near the campsite by chopper, especially in the dark. And I wasn't sure how the dogs would work, what with the smoke filled air and fires nearby. It wasn't exactly the kind of situation you could train for. I probably cursed when they told me it would take close to three hours to get there by jeep and on foot. Mrs. Barstow wanted to come, but there was no room in the jeep, what with me, Macauley, my dogs and our gear. It was just as well."

*"You'd best stay here, ma'am. We'll get your family back to you just as quick as we can."*

"And I prayed that I was doing the right thing, because somewhere deep inside me I knew damn well that I was lying."

---

Kristian looked up at her friend across the table. Maureen waited for her to continue her narrative.

"... but the fear and the tension were getting to me, and I decided that I needed something stronger than coffee, so I pushed Jesse off my lap and started to get up to go to the liquor cabinet. A nice glass of wine, perhaps with a Scotch chaser, was definitely in order. But just as I turned to head into the den, I caught something out of the corner of my eye that brought me back.

"There, on the screen, big as life, were pictures of the fire out in Wyoming. A reporter was saying something in the background, but the words didn't make much sense to me at the time. I was mesmerized by the footage of the towering flames and billowing smoke and burning trees and, for a moment, I thought I would lose it. Then a shiver ran through me, and somehow I knew that I would make it.

"I also knew that the man I loved more deeply than life itself wouldn't be coming home from this one."

Andersen brightened. "But that didn't happen. I mean, he did come home."

Kristian looked at her friend without speaking. Her lip quivered. "No, he didn't."

———— ⚬⚬⚬ ————

*Sheriff Dugan sets his dogs to finding a track, but he is afraid to let both dogs loose in the dark. Instead, he keeps one dog, Jackson, harnessed and on a rope. He lets Ricki search free.*

Ricki was his honey and best tracker and Jackson was almost as good. He tried not to influence Jackson on the rope, but he just did not have the same calm confidence that Mr. Travis had. Dugan was afraid that once either one of them got a scent, they'd both be gone. He couldn't afford to take that chance.

The two dogs scurried around hunting for a scent. Jackson cast from side to side like a beacon in the night, drifting to the northwest. Ricki ran in tight little circles, a little whirlwind in the mountain forest, working her way to the southeast.  Sure enough, as soon as Ricki picked up on something she let out a few quick barks and was gone in the night.

"What do you think, Mick?"

"Don't have a choice. Check the bearing and leave a note for the others."

"Good idea."

Thurston checked the direction and pinned a note to the tent opening. Dugan started the harnessed dog on the trail.

"I make it east-southeast," Thurston told him.

"Leastwise we seem to be on some sort of trail."

The bad news was they were heading for the fire.

Less than an hour later Dugan and Thurston could see flames and taste smoke. The wind was terrible, especially when it shifted and brought with it a pocket of smoke and heat, and the fire was worse than Thurston had expected. A roaring wall of flame towered to the smoke filled sky. At times, the heat was almost unbearable. Both men developed first degree burns. Jackson was hot on Ricki's trail. He made a forty-five degree turn to the left and the two men began climbing the steep slope to the east.

"Thiel Lake should be somewhere around here," Thurston shouted. "Could be good news."

"Hope so."

It wasn't.

From an elevation of 9,200 feet the two men got their first good view of the fires. The mountain air temperature here was forty-three degrees. Both men were sweating from the fire, now they were chilled.

"Damn," was all Thurston had to say. Dugan stood silent. The two northern fires had linked up as expected. They now formed a continuous bank of fire north of Upper Granite Lake starting just west of Thiel Lake and stretching almost two miles to the west. But the most immediate threat was still the spot fire they had just circumvented.

"Which way are they burning?" Dugan asked.

Thurston studied the situation for a second.

"Topography says northeast, wind says south."

"Which is it, Hank?"

Thurston considered a moment longer.

"Both. Look!"

From their vantage point the men could see the fires burning miles away to the southwest in addition to the ones close by in the north. They could not see the one by Native Lake, but they knew it was there.

"Let's get moving."

Jackson was still on track; there was no doubt about it. He pulled

Dugan along the south shore of Thiel Lake half the length of the lake. The sheriff and the ranger hoped they would run into the kids and their dad near the lake. They shouted at the top of their lungs to be heard above the tandem roars of wind and flame. All the men got for their efforts were sore throats and smoke filled chests.

"Pace yourself, Mick. We keep going in this direction and we got another climb to look forward to."

"Great."

"Take a drink and refill from the lake."

"Right."

The two men drank thirstily from their canteens. They automatically removed their hats and poured the rest of their water over their heads, aware for the first time how unusually hot they were for ten o'clock at night at 9000 feet. They filled their jugs with lake water, dropped in a few Halazone tablets, and moved on. A short distance further the dog in the lead made another sharp turn to the left.

"Where we headed now?"

"I make it to be back west."

"Least we're running with the contour."

"Yeah, but there ain't much of a trail."

They followed the contour of the slope through scrubby junipers and mountain pine. The vegetation wasn't thick, but it was brittle dry. It wouldn't take much to burn over the entire area.

Twenty-five minutes later and five hundred feet below, the team intersected the Upper Granite Lake Trail. Both men got excited when they heard a dog barking.

A dog barking to beat the band.

The team had been traveling west, more or less, following the contour of the mountain and the scent of Ricki. Now they followed one more sharp curve, almost one hundred-and-thirty degrees to the left. The new trail led them back to the southeast and down.

"This way, Hank," Mick Dugan shouted, breaking into a controlled jog. Jackson was pulling hard.

Hank Thurston was beginning to tire. He was glad to be going downhill, but he knew there was a problem.

"We're heading back to the camp."

Dugan didn't reply. He could hear his other dog clearly now, coming to him on wind and smoke. They picked up their pace, as best they could, and caught up with Ricki, deep in the forest, barking and sniffing and scampering from side to side and back and forth in a small area. *(I was right, Ricki knows but can express only with her actions. I knew I was on the right track. Can't you see? They were here!)*

Thurston and Dugan held up and shined their lights. There was something different here, but exactly what wasn't clear. The needles and cones and general debris on the ground were somehow different, disturbed, like a deer maybe had made its bed, or perhaps some other animal had been rooting around. Or maybe it had just been messed up by the excited dog they have caught up to, who herself was caught up in her own enthusiasm. *(They were here! They were here! Maybe they even stopped and rested for a spell, but dang if they weren't for sure here! Can't you see? We are on the right track! Let's go!)*

*Ricki spins one more time and starts off again, hesitating only once to stop and bark for Jackson and the men he is with to follow her. Jackson knows too and he leans into the tracking harness, momentarily pulling the sheriff off balance.*

Sheriff Dugan and Hank Thurston continued to follow Dugan's dogs, but Dugan was puzzled. He knew they were headed back to the campsite. He prayed they would find the missing people there, or at least some indication that they had recently been there. The fires were catching up and closing in. Smoke was making it harder and harder to breath, even wearing masks, which also made it hard to see. If the missing people weren't at the camp, Dugan was out of moves. Then the two men heard something that set their heart to racing.

*Ricki is barking again. So is Jackson. This time it is different. Sheriff Dugan knows that bark. They are barking at something or someone. This time the two men hear people talking.*

*Gogyeng Sowuhti knows that the time has come. Now it is up to the Shoshone and White Wind and the Son of Light. Gogyeng Sowuhti prays for them all.*

*By 9:00 p.m. expanding fires were advancing from two directions well into the Shoshone National Forest.*

# Chapter Twenty-four

*For Travis and Macauley, the night comes on with no perceptible difference other than thicker smoke and higher winds. The fires have grown to over seven thousand acres and are spreading fast in three directions. Laura Miller is in sporadic radio contact with the fire crews via the spotter plane. Arthur Marshall searches his maps and his mind for another place to try to make a stand.*

*The firefighters work feverishly, digging and scraping and raking the four foot wide trench down to mineral soil; praying against all evidence and experience that the fire-line will hold.*

*Sheriff Dugan and Hank Thurston head back to the campsite, worried and disappointed and pretty sure they're going the right way.*

*Guy Macauley and Joshua Travis and the dogs bang down the Muddy Creek trail in Miller's Forestry Service jeep. Joshua tries to take note of direction and landmarks, but it's too damn dark to see much of anything despite the ominous glow in the distance. He wonders how Macauley knows where the hell they are going.*

*Three miles and fifteen minutes later they are on foot, having gone as far as possible in the jeep.*

*Dr. Carolyn Barstow sits alone in a corner of the ranger station, waiting and crying and praying.*

*Kristian lights another cigarette and has another drink.*

*The good people of Cody, Wyoming and Red Lodge, Montana look out their windows at the ominous glow in the distance. They are worried about the direction of the fires and their loved ones on the line as they tuck their children into bed and kiss them goodnight.*

*And two teenagers and their father are out in that dangerous night, lost as hell.*

"Guy Macauley was a good man, Jon. He pushed that ol' jeep to its limit and then some, and he got us deeper into the forest than I would have thought possible. He drove very deliberately, picking his path carefully, but his concern was for us, not the vehicle. He said we should have seen him in 'Nam, before he had a wife and kids and got to doing things careful like. Good sense of humor. Good man.

"We came to Dugan's Blazer and Guy cursed, saying he could get us in another half mile in the jeep. The Blazer was too big. Then he got out and gunned that dang Blazer into the thick brush so's it was almost buried, but it was out of the way."

*"That'll teach Mick to park in the middle of the road."*

"He joked as he got back into the jeep, and I'll be a sonofagun if he didn't get us in another thousand yards, or so, before we bottomed out and broke an axle.

"We hoofed it in the rest of the way, and I sure hoped Macauley knew where we were going, because in some places the trail wasn't much more than a deer path. But after about two hours or so of hauling the mail we saw the lights of the campsite that Dugan and Thurston had rigged. Good thinking on their part."

"Good men."

Joshua nodded and sipped his drink.

"We shined our lights around the campsite and took our bearings. I tried to get a feel for the place and to decide what to do next. The winds were strong and shifting, and my eyes were tearing, and my lungs were choking from all the smoke in the air. It was hotter than hell, and I wasn't acclimated to the altitude. I was winded and lightheaded from the get-go. We tried to contact Dugan with the walkie-talkie, but it was no good. All we got was crackling static. Then Macauley called to me."

*"Mr. Travis, look at this!"*

"I walked over to one of the tents. There on the flap, with a lantern propped up to shine right on it, was a message written in black marker."

**9:07 – ESE 110° Dugan**

"Good thinking."

"Damn right. Those people were all right, every one of 'em. Then I started thinking maybe we could pull this off after all. I only wished it was the father, and not just the sheriff, that was telling us what direction he was heading."

*The big man from Wisconsin puts down his gear and gets to work searching the tents for articles to give his dogs the scent. He moves carefully and deliberately, not wanting to make a mistake. Not tonight. He wants to make sure he uses things touched only by the kids. Anything scented by the mother, or even the father, might throw them off in the wrong direction.*

*The deputy keeps trying to raise the sheriff or the ranger base on the radios, but it isn't going to happen. Too many mountains, too many trees, bad atmospherics.*

*The tracker finds some underwear and some sneakers in each tent. He hopes they belong to the kids. He doesn't know whether Dugan has handled them, but he decides to take a chance. Then he sees a second note that says **Kid's bag**. He doesn't take time to figure it out or to second guess. Just more good thinking, he reasons. Suddenly, he hears barking and shouting outside!*

"Guy was shouting for me and at someone else. Jenny-Dog and Ellie were barking up a storm. I crawled out the tent opening and saw two men wearing smoke masks over their faces, straining to hold back two large dogs that were spinning and straining to get to my two dogs who were standing and barking and needing every bit of their will power not to break the *stay* I had put them at. One man was wearing a miner's helmet. He was helping the other who wore a Forest Service hat, a baseball cap, not a Smokey the Bear hat. When the men removed the masks, I saw that the one with the miner's helmet was Mick Dugan, the man I had met at Jenny Lake the year before. The other turned out to be Hank Thurston, the supervising ranger for that region. I looked around quickly, then at the men, who were in pretty rough shape, but we were out of luck. Neither the kids nor the father were with them.

"It was up to us."

*He goes over to the sheriff, who is kneeling on one knee coughing, and to the other man who is exhausted, dehydrated, and nearly overpowered by the smoke despite the mask. He must shout to be heard above the roar of the wind and the fire. After a few words, the man from Wisconsin takes one mask and hangs it around his neck without putting it over his face. Macauley takes the other. The extra masks might come in handy if they find the missing family. Joshua takes the articles he has chosen and the sleeping bag over to Jenny-Dog and Ellie and has them take the scent.*

*The dogs start working the ground and the air, mostly the ground. The smoke filled air makes them sneeze and shake their heads and the dogs crouch and wriggle and back-step in unusual ways as they try to find the trail. Ellie works towards the east then suddenly barks and spins and rolls on the ground and Joshua knows she has found the trail. Dugan's dogs are more excited than ever.*

*Jenny-Dog races over to see what Ellie has found, but she doesn't start spinning and barking and getting excited as Joshua expects her to.*

*Instead, she works back over towards the path they have come in on, and it is here that Jenny starts barking and indicating for the man to follow.*

*"What do you think?" he asks the sheriff.*

*"Damned if I know. We could've missed something on a night like this, that's for damn sure."*

*"Maybe that black dog is on the mother's trail," Thurston suggests. "Or has picked up ours."*

*"Or maybe she's just smart enough to tell us we'd all best get our asses outta here," Macauley puts in. The fire is now in sight, moving down on them quickly from two directions.*

*Joshua looks at Jenny, then at Ellie. Then he looks past Ellie, deep into the forest. He can see the approaching fire. He thinks about it for a minute.*

*"You followed that track to the east?" Joshua asks.*

*"That's right," Dugan confirms, "then a big loop around to the north and west and then back to here. Came to one spot that seemed fussed up a bit and the dogs went crazy, but then they brought us back here."*

*Joshua puzzles over it for another moment. Then it comes to him.*

*"You didn't miss anything," he tells the sheriff as he moves to harness up Ellie. He sends Jenny-Dog out into the burning night to find the kids and, hopefully, the father.*

"You wait here for Dog Man then go home," Son of Light tells the Shoshone guide.

"We go together," the Shoshone replies. "You don't know the way."

"I'll follow White Wind," Son of Light tells him.

"We go together."

*The fires were jumping and spotting as swirling wind and vertical convection columns carried burning cones and branches high into the air only to fall back to earth and to start new fires. The new fires then linked up and trapped all life between them and the main fires.*

# Chapter Twenty-five

*The fire supervisor checks the map again, then sighs woefully. The winds are so high they can't use the aircraft to drop water or retardant, couldn't even if it was daylight.*

*The teams from Minnesota and Prescott, fighting the Granite Lake fire, have to retreat to their safety zones and are evacuated by truck.*

*In Cody, the people sleep and pray.*

*Near Merrill, Wisconsin, Kristian lights another cigarette and throws back another Scotch. She should have passed out by now. Instead, she's wired awake as she flicks the remote, looking for some more news.*

*On the ground, the would-be rescuers move out.*

"We headed out along the same path we had come in on. Jenny was long gone and on the loose. Ellie was next, pulling hard on the lead rope. Guy Macauley was right behind me followed by Dugan who was trying to hold back his dogs and help the exhausted ranger at the same time. I think the ranger was experiencing chest pains too. He kept clutching his left shoulder.

"That night was a bad one to be out in those woods, Jon, even without the fire. I guessed the wind at about 25 to 30 miles per hour with swirling gusts a lot higher and short intermittent lulls. The long dry summer had taken its toll on the trees, and the wind was bringing down lots of snags and widowmakers.

"The summer had made the woods flammable as matchsticks, and the fire was moving almost as fast as we were. The smoke was bad and the heat made your lungs burn, but the worst thing was that the fire was jumping around. The wind was carrying flaming branches and embers dozens of yards at a time, starting new fires where they landed on the ground debris and in the crowns. We knew that if the fire landed near the vehicles or cut us off, we would be in a real jam. They would go up in an instant, and we would be cut off from the main trail.

"We moved along the path back towards the busted jeep and the hidden Blazer. If we got to the vehicles without the kids and Jenny was waiting for us, that would be all she wrote. We kept looking over our shoulders at the approaching fire and all I could think to say was, *Shit!* What I didn't know at the time was that there was another fire that had blown up and was heading towards us from the southwest."

"Would it have made a difference if you had known?"

Joshua pondered the question for a moment then he responded, "Not likely. Not long after we left the camp, a half-hour, maybe less, we caught up with Jenny-Dog at a fork in the path. *(Jenny-Dog is puzzled. She knows she is on the right track, but the right track ends. She backtracks a bit and checks again. Yes, she knows, this is the right track. But wait… There are two right tracks. How can that be?)* Jenny-Dog was scurrying all over the place, confused. First she would head towards the south and we would get ready to follow. Then she would change her mind and come back, checking all around with her nose on the ground and in the air. Finally she decided and headed down the right branch, to the west. Macauley pulled on my arm and stopped us."

*"The vehicles are down this way," he shouts, pointing to the left.*

"I paused for a moment, but my heart was pounding. There it was. The pieces were coming together like a Sherlock Holmes mystery. I couldn't be sure but I guessed that the kids must have first wandered off to the east, leaving the trail that Dugan had followed. At some point, they must have wound their way around to the north and northwest. Eventually, they found their way back to the campsite, coming in on the northwest side of the site and finding their waiting father. Dugan's dogs, and Ellie too, had picked up the most unambiguous track based on the scents they were given. But ol' Jenny-Dog, God love her, knew something was wrong and by gosh if she didn't pick out the right track through all the covering scents of all of us hiking in. The kids and their dad most likely started hiking out on the path that we were on now, the one that led to the road and the ranger station, but at this point, either by mistake or by design, they had chosen the trail to the west."

"Damn," VanStavern commented, "helluva price to pay for a simple mistake."

Joshua frowned.

*"Are you sure?" Joshua asks, but he knows that the deputy is right. Macauley just looks at him and nods.*

*"Where does this one lead?" Travis asks.*

*"Who the hell knows. Should be the stream bed, all dried up and overgrown. Too soon to be Copeland Trail. Maybe leads back towards the fire but eventually should come down and around to the lake, if we can make it that far. No way of tellin' for sure, but if I was lookin' for a safety zone, I might chance it."*

*"It was decision time, Jon. So I decided. As God is my witness, I decided."*

*"Wait for Thurston and Dugan, then get the hell outta here. I'll see if I can find 'em and get 'em out! Wait for us by the Blazer as long as you can, then get the hell outta here whether we're back or not!"*

*"You're gonna need help gettin' them folks outta there. 'Specially if one or more of 'em is down!"*

*"I'll be all right."*

*Dugan and Thurston catch up.*

*"You don't know this area like I do, Mr. Travis. I might come in handy if you get turned around or cut off by the fire!"*

"I knew he was right, Jon, but I had this bad feeling that I just couldn't shake. I wasn't trying to be a hero or anything. I just didn't want to risk any more lives than was absolutely necessary."

*"You don't have a hard hat."*

*"We wear Stetsons around here, t' cover our hard heads. And hell, a little smoke don't bother me none. I seen worse, burnin' leaves in autumn."*

"Of course, I knew his bravado was bullshit. He knew the risks better than anyone. Even so, I liked it."

*"Whattaya think, Mick?" Macauley asks Dugan.*

"Suddenly we heard unexpected sounds coming from the northeast, metallic sounds and chain saw sounds and the sounds of human voices."

"Must be the Boise team,"Thurston advised,"down from Hidden Lake. Maybe the Barstows have hooked up with them."

"I knew it was a longshot, especially with Jenny-Dog off to the west. It would have been stupid not to check, but it would also waste time if they weren't there. *Are your radios working?* I asked the sheriff and his deputy."

*"Hit and miss," Dugan replies. "We can probably reach each other. Don't know about Command."*

*"Tell you what," Joshua tells Dugan, "give me a radio. You three check out the fire team. I'll follow my dog. If we don't find anything, we'll come back"*

*"No way!" Dugan objects. "Guy and Hank can touch base with the team. I'm going with you."*

*"Hold on there, Mick," now it's Macauley's turn to put in his two cents, "you and Hank been running around out here for hours. Give someone else a chance to play."*

"Macauley wasn't really trying to make light of the situation. He knew that Dugan and Thurston had to be beat. Thurston was kneeling again. He knew it was time to bring in fresh legs.

"Dugan, on the other hand, was reluctant to send a subordinate into harm's way when he himself was available. Maybe it wasn't my place, Jon, but I finally stepped in."

*"Gentlemen, we're wasting valuable time. Who knows the area best?" Joshua demands.*

*Dugan grudgingly admits it is Macauley who is most familiar with the terrain, more familiar even than the ranger.*

*Dugan unhappily relinquishes command to the man he has called in to help. "It's your call, Mr. Travis. It's your ball game now. You got the masks."*

"I looked at Guy Macauley. He was a good man, all right. I knew I should have him along. But on the other hand, I sure didn't want to lose him. You see, Jon, the bottom line was did I think I would find the kids; and what condition would they be in even if I did? I looked at Ellie and into the woods. I looked at the fires, that I knew would be on both sides of us, and then back at Ellie. All my instincts told me to cut our losses while we still could, but I couldn't operate like that. I couldn't live with myself if I did, especially knowing Jenny was out front and on track."

*"You two hook up with the fire team. Call us if the Barstows are there and call us if you have any new info on the fires. Then get the hell out, if you can, or at least get to a safe area. We'll follow Jenny-Dog."*

"I looked at Macauley again."

*"Let's go!"*

*They chase down the right fork. It's narrow and overgrown, not all that different from the other trail in the dark, and it curves and winds down a steep hill until they are moving roughly perpendicular to their original track and parallel to the approaching blaze in the north, directly towards the Lost Lake blowup that has now spread to envelop both the southern and southeastern shores of lower Granite Lake. They hit another track at the bottom of a gulch that heads them back to the northwest. Macauley stops him for a moment. He tries the walkie-talkie. No good.*

*"We're heading towards the lake!" he shouts. "Might have a chance if we find 'em there, but if the fire jumps us we'll be cut off!"*

*"How far?"*

*"Can't say for sure. Mile or two maybe. Maybe less. Rough terrain!"*

"*Shit*, I thought as we got moving again, that meant maybe an hour or more the way we were going, and I didn't think the fire would stay off us that long.

"Ellie was pulling hard and confident. That was good because it meant we were trailing Jenny close, and I had learned over the years to trust Jenny-Dog.

"The wind was as bad as ever, fanning the fire towards us and bringing down lots of dead wood. The roaring and howling sounded like a damn freight train that was up close and moving fast, and the creaking and crashing noises were louder than hell and just as eerie, but it was the worst when the wind shifted for a moment, because that was when the smoke and gases caught us full on and made it impossible to see and near impossible to breathe."

*"Hit the deck!" Macauley orders. "Breathe close to the ground and be ready to move!"*

*As soon as the smoke and gasses lift, Macauley shouts, "Now!"*

*The two men and one dog are up and running once again.*

"We hustled through those woods as best we could, Jon, but I was huffing like a freshman doing wind sprints up Wheaton Hill and I could feel my heart pounding. I just couldn't get the oxygen I needed. My legs were wobbly and my sides ached. We both had dampened neckerchiefs tied over our nose and mouth to keep out the smoke. We had tried the masks, but they fogged up and made it impossible to see, so we went with dampened neckerchiefs. They seemed to be doing the trick, for the most part, and I prayed that the people we were looking for had thought to do the same. Then Ellie led us up the west side of the gulch and along the contour just below the ridge. She found a break in the ridge rock and took us through it, and damn if another fire wasn't right there."

*The fire lights up the area, but time races by. They stumble through brush and slip on rocks in the jagged terrain along the ridge. The two men have no idea how long they have been on the trail. It seems like forever, and the fires are getting too damn close and jumping over them in spots.*

*They come to the top of a rise. Ellie pauses for a second. Then she leans hard into the harness and pulls down towards another gulch. There is no doubt in her mind.*

"It was hard to hear much in that firestorm. The wind and flames roared like a plane engine winding up, and the smoke was worse than when we were kids standing on the Orchard Road bridge with a steam locomotive belching four feet beneath us. But I thought I heard something that made my heart leap.

"Ellie started barking and pulling as hard as she could. Sure enough, on the other side of the gulch, less than half way to the top of the hill was Jenny-Dog, barking and whining and licking the faces of the three people we were looking for. But we were too late, Jon. All three were down."

*The guide the Shoshone People had sent was also a medicine man. A medicine man with powerful magic. His magic could bring people back from the dead.*

*Then the Shoshone medicine man left the Son of Light.*

*Sometimes the areas between fires can be superheated above the point of ignition. A fresh charge of oxygen, whether from wind or convection, can cause a blowup. Not many people have ever survived a blowup.*

# Chapter Twenty-six

*Craig Barstow and the two teenagers have traveled as fast and as far as they can, but it is no good. Altitude and noxious gasses work together to deny their muscles much needed oxygen. Lactic acid builds up in the muscles but cannot dissipate. First their legs and feet give out and they fall to the ground. Next their chests and their diaphragms give out as they pass into a world of swirling time and light and colors and memories....*

*Joshua and Macauley shine their lights and see the man and the girl lying together. A few feet away lies the boy. All three are pointing uphill. All three have burned out flashlights. A bolt action rifle is slung over the man's shoulder. Compasses are on the ground.*

*The man from Wisconsin and the deputy from Wyoming spring into coordinated action without a word. Joshua checks the man and the teenage girl, looking for signs of life. Guy Macauley checks the boy. The bodies are still warm and supple, but neither rescuer can find a single pulse. They begin CPR anyway. The fire is now yards away.*

"I rolled the man off his daughter and started to give her CPR. I knew in my heart she was dead, but I couldn't not try. Right? Finally I gave up and tried the man, but that was no use either. I was sick about being too late. I couldn't stop trying to revive the father and the daughter, bouncing back and forth between them. I hyperventilated and fell back on my butt.

"I could hear the dogs barking and feel them licking me, but I couldn't do anything. Then I felt cool water running over my face and my eyes, and that brought me to. I saw Guy Macauley kneeling over me with a canteen in one hand."

All this was new to VanStavern.

"I nodded and he winked and moved quickly back to the boy to resume CPR. I crawled over to them and squatted by them for a couple of seconds. It was time for us to beat it the hell out of there. The fire was almost on top of us, and we were being cut off. If we waited much longer we would be boxed in. The heat was tremendous, probably around a hundred and twenty, hundred and thirty, maybe more, and I saw no signs of life.

"I had to shout to be heard above the fire."

*"What's the deal, buddy?"*

"I asked Macauley. I figured it was his call. He had to be the one to let it go."

*"He's alive."*

"He told me, never stopping the chest compressions he was doing.

"I was stunned shitless. I couldn't believe it. I knew he had to be wrong – confusing hope with reality. I checked for a pulse under the boy's jaw. I felt none, so I put my hand on Guy's shoulder."

*"It's time to get out of here."*

*"He's alive, man!" Macauley snaps back. "Give me a hand!"*

"It was crazy. Utter madness! I should have dragged him away. Instead, I knelt down across from him, and we switched to two-man CPR."

*The two men work on the boy, ever mindful of the fire that is almost on top of them. The brush at the top of the gulch is already burning, and the wind is pushing the fire their way, topography notwithstanding. But the air where they are is still clear, or at least clear enough for them to breathe.*

*Joshua knows he will have to be the one to make the decision to leave the boy, and he knows he will have to make it damn soon. He's about to say the word when suddenly he feels the body he is pressing on move ever so slightly. A small jerk, more like a shudder, sends a thrill through him like a bass checking out a popper on four pound test. The boy is either coming to or he is dying.*

"A few seconds later, the boy began coughing first and then retching. Guy rolled the boy on his side and cleared the vomit from the kid's mouth with his fingers. I poured some water on the boy's forehead and cheeks and the back of his neck. I couldn't believe it. As far as I'm concerned, Guy Macauley brought that boy back from the dead. Now we had to keep him alive. Him and us."

Jonathan listened in silence. He knew what was coming.

"We had to get the hell out of there. The boy was coming around, but he was still very weak. We wanted to take things slow so's he wouldn't slip into shock, but we couldn't. The fire was setting the pace."

*"We're going to get you out of here, son," Joshua tells him, trying to sound calm and to mask the fear that he feels. "Just relax and let us do all the work."*

*"Dad?" the boy creaks out.*

*"Don't worry about them." He doesn't know what else to say. "Just try to relax and breathe. We're going to put a gas mask on you just in case the smoke gets thick again."*

"The gas mask was too big to make a tight fit so we sealed it by putting a damp neckerchief over his head and tying it off with another one. I hoisted the boy up across my shoulders in a fireman's carry. It was time to split. Macauley tried the radio one more time, but all he got was crackling static."

*"Which way now?" he asks Macauley. They don't need to climb out of the gully to know they are cut off.*

*"Let's try and make it to the lake. It shouldn't be far."*

"It made sense to me. We were cut off. Outracing that fire through thick brush and woods would have been impossible. The lake at least gave us some options and a fighting chance. We hoped the cool water would help make the smoke rise and maybe keep it off us. I reckoned that if there was enough of a shore and the wind was right, we might even be able to keep ahead of the fire, or at least wait it out in relative safety.

"I lost track of Guy for a moment. I looked around for him quickly, wanting him to take the lead. There wasn't a damn moment to lose. But before we got down to the business of saving our own hides Guy had one more thing to do."

*The man from Wisconsin sees the deputy unload the rifle and slip the clip into his pocket. He then swallows hard as he watches Guy Macauley arrange the bodies of the young girl and her father in a loving embrace, waiting together to be carried to eternity.*

*The deputy scurries back, picks up Joshua's backpack and rope, and takes the lead. From across the big man's shoulders, the boy is just conscious enough to catch a glimpse of the embracing pair.*

*Neither man has noticed the Ace bandage tightly wrapped around the girl's injured ankle. An injury that has slowed the family down just enough...*

"I wasn't sure if the boy was conscious or not, but I knew he was alive. It was something you could just feel."

VanStavern nodded.

"We moved along as quickly as we could, but we had to move carefully. There were lots of loose stones and dead wood and brush. The fire was lighting our way pretty good, but the smoke blinded us and choked our throats, and the heat burned our lungs something awful. Both dogs were off lead, and I wasn't always sure just where they were. But I couldn't be worried about that. They could watch out for themselves, I figured.

"We followed the contour north as it wound around for another quarter-mile or so. Then we came around one last curve and stopped dead in our tracks. We were dumbfounded. We couldn't believe what we saw."

*There it is, big as life and closer than either of them had dared hope. The high mountain lake.*

*The two men look at each other in utter amazement and disbelief. Then it strikes both of them, just how close the lost campers had come to making it and what a raw, dirty deal they had been dealt. The impact is staggering and sobering, and Guy Macauley sums it all up when he looks back at Joshua and says softly, almost under his breath, "Damn!"*

"But we weren't out of the woods yet. We had to decide how to escape the fire. I asked Guy about wading along the shore, but he said we couldn't move fast enough through the brush where it came down to the lake, and that the lake edge dropped off sharp and deep and we would wind up swimming for it.

"That wasn't a good prospect. Hell, I'm a pretty fair swimmer, Jon, you know that, but that wind had that lake whipped into a froth, and I knew it was bound to be cold. We wouldn't have had much of a chance, especially toting that boy like we were."

*"What do you think about clearing some of this brush out and waiting it out right here," Macauley suggests, "even if we have to sit in the water for a spell?"*

"I looked around. I didn't like it." Joshua shook his head. "The shore area was small and narrow and we'd have to clear a helluva lot of brush in a small amount of time. Even doing that, some of the trees were exploding, and there was no telling which way the trees and branches on the hillside would fall. Shoot, there were already some good size trees we could see that had crashed into the lake. And that fire had to be sucking up oxygen. And on top of all that, I didn't think we could last too long hanging around in that lake that night, especially the kid. The water was too rough and too cold, even with the surrounding fire."

*"We need to get away from the fire," Joshua tells the deputy. "If we chance it out here we gotta beat burning in the fire, hypothermia or drowning in the water, or suffocating to death if the wind goes wrong."*

"That's what I figured must have happened to the man and the girl."

*"Yeah, maybe. Too bad we don't have a boat."*

"I looked at him and looked around and then back at him as I thought a moment. Damn, if he hadn't come up with the answer again."

*"Let's make a raft!"*

*The two men check the boy, then leave him with the dogs near (but not too near) the lake edge, under a solar blanket. They go to work like a well-drilled team; Joshua with the sharp hand ax he has brought and Macauley using a knife to cut lengths of rope from the coil hanging on the backpack and the dogs' lead rope.*

*They work quickly but deliberately, fearing mistakes more than the creeping exhaustion. But the fire is still setting the driving pace.*

*Joshua chops dead or dying trees, cutting eight-foot logs no more than eight inches across. His athletic strength and practiced deftness with an ax make it look easy. Guy finishes with the rope and starts searching for live, flat boughs to be used for a platform. Things are going pretty smoothly. After the first three logs are cut, Macauley taps Joshua on the shoulder.*

*"How are you at lashings?" Macauley asks.*

*Joshua hands him the ax.*

*"We need two more logs and some more green boughs."*

*They set the two biggest logs parallel to each other, maybe six feet apart. Three thinner logs are lashed across, forming a deck. Flat green branches are woven and tied into the deck to give them something to sit on. It isn't pretty, but it should hold and not capsize.*

*Macauley brings in the last logs just as Joshua finishes lashing the first ones together.*

"Guy brought in the last of the green stuff and checked the kid. We both worked on making the platform good enough to sit on for a spell – maybe for hours. We were almost done, and I sent Guy out to find a long push pole. I finished the raft and tied a rope across the top to hang onto. Then I set the backpack dead center on the raft and attached it to the rope, straps up. I checked on the kid and brought him over to the raft. He was still pretty disoriented, but I didn't think it was shock, at least not in the medical meaning of the word.

"I looked around for Guy, wishing he'd get back right quick. The fire was just about on us, and the wind had died down a tad. I wanted to shove off.

"I waited a couple more minutes and shouted a few times, but I still couldn't see him. *Oh shit!* I thought as a feeling came over me that made me want to sink down and cry. But there wasn't time for that kind of noise. Not then.

"I told Ellie to stay with the boy and the boy to stay put. Then I sent Jenny out to find Macauley. I wished I'd saved some rope for the harness lead, but I'd used it all on the raft. I figured he couldn't be far and Jenny would bark, so I sent her out loose.

"I was right. Moments later I heard Jenny-Dog barking away, and when I saw the spot fire near where I heard her, I got scared. But when I ran over to her and found Guy Macauley, I got sick."

*Guy Macauley is lying face down on the ground in a grotesque sort of spread-eagle. The treetop that has snapped his neck and caved in part of his skull is lying across him and still burning. Jenny is barking and nudging the body. Joshua doesn't have to touch him to know he is dead – but he does.*

*Damn, he thinks, this widowmaker has sure been true to its name.*

*"Remember how our people emerged from the Third World into the Fourth World. You must go through the water," Gogyeng Sowuhti tells the Son of Light. "Emerge from Topqolu back into the Fourth World."*

*By midnight ten thousand acres were ablaze. By 3:00 a.m. the fires encompassed almost thirteen thousand acres, incinerating everything in their paths. Then things began to change.*

# Chapter Twenty-seven

Jonathan VanStavern sat in stunned silence. He had known Macauley had died. He had even known some of the details. Now he understood the full impact this man's death had had on his friend.

"I felt queasy and like I might mess myself. If I had eaten more that day I probably would have.

"The ax lay a foot or so from his hand. I picked it up and finished working on the felled sapling Guy had chosen for the push pole. As I worked, I thought how his head didn't look so dang hard now, and that now it was three down and two to go, not counting the dogs. The fire had already won. The only thing left to decide would be by how much.

"I looked at Macauley one last time before heading back to the raft with the pole. I hated to leave him like that but what else could I do? It would have meant too much time and too much space to tie him on the raft. And he wasn't a pretty sight. The kid sure didn't need to see him like that and neither did anybody else, so I left him. God, Jonathan, I just left him. I didn't even think to pick up his damn Stetson."

"Nothing else you could've done."

There is a hitch in Joshua's voice as he tells his friend the story, "Nope, nothing."

VanStavern doesn't have to look at him to know that there are tears on his cheeks.

*The man and the dog return to the boy and the raft. He lays the push pole down and tries to get the raft into the water. It's heavier than he thought and hung up on a small rock. He clears the rock and tries again, lifting and pushing first one corner then another. He wades into the water and tries lifting and pulling. Grudgingly, the raft begins to budge, and step by step he is able to walk it towards the water until finally one log is almost completely in the lake and begins to rise.*

"I lay the pole across one end of the raft and set the dogs on the deck, one on each side of the backpack. I told them *down* and *stay* and hoped, for all our sakes, they'd be able to hold it. I got the boy and told him it was time to go."

*"Where's the other man?"*

*"He's dead. Now it's just us."*

"I probably should have said it better, but at the time I just couldn't think how.

"It was hotter than hell. Trees were burning and falling into the gully and the nearby brush was starting to catch. Embers were landing close by, popping and hissing when they hit the water.

"I placed the boy, chest down, over the backpack and slipped his arms through the shoulder straps. That way he wouldn't go far even if he fell asleep or passed out. I told him to grab hold of the cross rope and he did. That was a good sign.

"I wished I'd had something to tie down the dogs, but we used all the rope for the lashings. Then I thought to use my belt for Jenny and the tracking harness for Ellie. We were set to go.

"I untied my boots but didn't take them off. The raft platform was hard on the feet, but I wanted to be able to get my boots off quick if we wound up in the water.

"I pushed and shoved the raft until one log was all the way in the water. Then it was easier. The raft was bobbing up and down with the waves pretty good, and I just had to time my shoves right. It felt like it would hold together and I didn't think she would capsize. I put my back into it and was able to lift and twist it around so's the second log was half in the water. One more shove would do it."

*"Here we go!" he shouts. The boy doesn't respond, but he sees him tighten his grip on the rope-hold.*

*Thatta boy.*

*He pushes the raft onto the dark, roiling lake. The fire lights the perimeter and glows red and yellow in the black water. He wades up to his knees then jumps aboard. Kneeling across from the boy, he calms the dogs with his voice and pushes the long pole deep into the water. He is amazed how quickly he can no longer reach bottom.*

"My game plan was to push out as far from shore as possible and let the wind and the lake carry us ahead of the fire. At first we kept drifting back to shore, and I kept having to pole us out again to keep us moving away from the fire, and eventually either the wind or the shore-line changed, and we floated out towards the center of the lake."

*"How you doin', son?"*

*"Okay."*

*"Hang tough."*

*"I will."*

"I hoped I could do the same. I could feel the fatigue and exhaustion setting in. Fatigue in my mind, exhaustion in my body. You know how it goes. I was wet and cold and nauseous, and I wondered what time it was and how long until first light. And as we swung around I looked into the burning forest that had already claimed at least three lives, and I wondered how long we could hang on out there.

"I remember thinking ol' Mother Nature can really be a mean bitch sometimes. Whole mountains were on fire, and I swear there were walls of flame shooting five hundred feet high. Sometimes the smoke was on the bottom and the flames were on top, high into the sky, and I wondered if Hell itself could be any worse than that night."

*They toss and drift and turn forever through the nightmare of burning trees and wind swept water. A man who hasn't slept for a day, a boy who saw his sister and father die, and two dogs all clinging to a makeshift raft that is the only thing between them and disaster.*

*The dogs whine and fidget, nervous and uncomfortable.*

*"Steady, guys," he tells them, in as calm a tone as he can muster. "Stay down."*

*The boy has fallen into a sobbing sleep. The man looks down on him and wonders if he has done him any favor.*

*The clouds and smoke and patches of stars swirl above as the man wishes it was over, almost not caring how. Only the thoughts of Kristian and the memories of Guy Macauley and the dead lips of the girl and her father keep him from giving in to the seductive temptation to give up.*

*He knows full well they are in God's hands now, and that their fate has been, quite literally, cast to the wind. But he'll be damned if he's going to roll over and die. Not after all that's happened and coming this far. That would be a betrayal of those who had died. And too damn easy to boot!*

*And when morning finally comes and the wind calms down and the lake flattens some, he doesn't even notice.*

"Hell, it wasn't until Jenny-Dog and Ellie started barking and whining did I see that it was getting light and the sun was almost up. I shook myself and tried to get my bearings. The lake was still bouncy but not near as bad as it had been. I was soaking wet and freezing cold. I looked around and saw that we were out in the middle somewhere, well away from the shores. There was fire to our south and fire to the east and northeast, but it didn't seem to be gaining on us. Hell, from out there it didn't even seem so threatening. Thousands of acres burning and it didn't seem threatening anymore. And I realized for the first time since we found the kid that we were going to make it.

"I rolled from my kneeling position, opposite the kid, to one on my back, propping myself up on my elbows. I was stiff as a board. I heard the rhythmic beating of a chopper and prayed it would see us. I looked at the boy and thought to myself, *that kid can sleep through anything.* Then panic set in."

*"Kid! Hey kid! Wake up!" he yells, shaking the boy. But he knows he is dead. Oh shit, he thinks, not you too! "C'mon kid! Wake up, damn it!" The helicopter is getting closer. "C'mon kid," he begs. "Please wake up," and he realizes that he hasn't even taken the time to learn the boy's name.*

"Out of the corner of my eye I could see the big Sikorski coming down towards the lake, but I didn't care. What was the damn point if the kid was dead?"

*The large helicopter comes down on the lake with its collapsible bucket and starts taking on water to be dumped on the still raging fire. The dogs are barking with excitement, trying to stand up and rocking the raft.*

*The man is preoccupied with the boy.*

*Finally, he sees the boy move and his heart races. There's a blink! Then an open eye followed by lots of blinking and squinting!*

*The man rolls back to a supine position, looks up at the sky and says a small prayer of Thanks.*

"I told God I owed Him one. Then I thought, damn, I must really be losing it if I can't tell when a kid is just sleeping.

"I looked across to the kid who was now awake but who was still lying across the backpack, clutching the rope-hold as he had all night."

*"What's your name, son?"*

*The helicopter takes off without seeing them. He tries the small radio again, but it's gotten wet and it's shot. Before the first chopper even dumps its load, a second one is coming in. This time he stands, carefully, on the bobbing evergreen platform, and waves his arms and flashlights. This time the crew sees them, and the chopper, after hovering above the water and retracting its giant ladle, turns and heads towards them.*

*The nightmare is almost over.*

*Gogyeng Sowuhti sent Spotted Eagle to rescue the Son of Light. Spotted Eagle carried a ladder made from reeds.*

*The wind was steady but calmed as it shifted back to the southwest. The fires continued to burn but they were headed in the right direction.*

# Chapter Twenty-eight

*On a small farm outside Merrill, Wisconsin a young woman, who hasn't slept all night, begins the morning chores her husband usually does.*

*Hank Thurston is in the hospital in Cody, Wyoming.*

*Mick Dugan, upon receiving word by radio, gets the Spirit Air helicopter to fly Mrs. Barstow to the airport at Cody.*

*On a small ranch in the Sunlight Basin, north of Cody, Wyoming, a young pregnant woman is sleeping with her daughter. In one hour she will fix breakfast for her ten-year-old son who will be proudly coming in from the morning chores he has taken care of all by himself. In two hours she will learn of the death of her husband.*

"It was tricky getting into that chopper from the raft. It was rigged with a winch and harness that they lowered off of a yardarm by the door, but it was still tricky, especially the kid and the dogs. We got on board and just lay back on the deck. None of us were any too steady, although I guess I had somehow managed to stand up on the raft to wave them in. The chopper flew us directly to the airport at Cody."

*"You the Barstows?" the crewman asks.*

*"He is," Travis replies.*

*"Thought you were all gonners. Weren't really lookin' for survivors."*

*Survivors, Joshua thinks, yep, that's what we are. Then he asks,*

*"Dugan and that ranger make it back okay?"*

*"They made it back. Evacuated with the fire team. I heard Hank Thurston's in the hospital, but I think he's okay."*

*Joshua gets to his knees. He half stands and makes it to a window. For the first time he sees the full magnitude of the inferno he and the boy have escaped.*

"Carolyn Barstow met us in Cody. That other chopper pilot, Littlejohn, must have ferried her down. Dugan was there also. That poor woman must have been torn between joy and grief. She kept hugging her son all the while looking and asking for her husband and her daughter.

"I was completely shot to hell. I was totally drained, physically and emotionally, but there was no one else to do it.

"I took this once beautiful and strong woman by the shoulders."

*"I'm sorry, ma'am but your husband and your daughter aren't coming back. We found them too late. They were already gone."*

"She looked at her son, and I could read all the questions in her eyes."

*"He was a gonner too, ma'am, but somehow Deputy Macauley brought him back." He watches it sink in then adds softly, "I'm sorry we didn't do better."*

*The woman knows she has to be strong as she helps her son to the waiting ambulance. She doesn't make it as she crumbles to her knees, crying uncontrollably.*

*Sheriff Dugan knows he has to be strong too as he girds himself to ask the dreaded question.*

*"What happened to Guy?"*

*The big man from Wisconsin looks at him.*

*"Widowmaker."*

*"You'd best ride into town with them and get yourself checked out at the hospital too," Dugan tells him.*

*Joshua has a lot of first and a few small second degree burns but he shakes him off.*

*"I'm all right. I just want to get cleaned up and get on home. Macauley have a wife?"*

*"And kids."*

*"I'll go with you to tell them."*

*"No. That's my job."*

"Somehow, it didn't seem right, Jon, but the fact of the matter is I was damn glad. I picked up my duffel that Dugan had brought down and looked for the dogs as I headed for the terminal to find a phone. I turned back and looked at Mick Dugan, who looked almost as beat as I was."

*"Sheriff, tell Mrs. Macauley that a man and a boy are alive today because of her husband."*

*"I will, Mr. Travis." Dugan starts to leave but he hesitates. "Mr. Travis..." the sheriff begins. He wants to say something more but can't get it out. "...thanks," is all he can manage.*

*It isn't enough.*

*"Masauwu, he has survived the challenge. He has passed the test. Now you must leave him alone and let me help him," Gogyeng Sowuhti cries.*

*"No, Grandmother," Skeleton Man replies. "He has survived only the fire. The test is just beginning."*

# Chapter Twenty-nine

Maureen Andersen sat in stunned silence. Her lips were parted, her eyes were wide and full of tears. Finally she was able to speak softly, "My God, Kristian, he must have been devastated."

Kristian was crying also. "That's putting it mildly. From the very first word I heard Joshua speak over the phone after that rescue, I knew that things were different. I was thrilled, of course, to hear from him and to know that he was safe, and I attributed my feeling of anxiety to lack of sleep. But deep inside I knew.

"I didn't know any of the details. Josh had only said that he was okay and that he had gotten one kid out. But I knew that something was terribly wrong and that this rescue hadn't been like any other.

"It took the better part of the day for them to find a plane that could fly Joshua and the dogs back to Wisconsin. Jonathan VanStavern picked me up, and we drove to the airport in Wausau where Josh was coming in. Some rich rancher was flying him home on his personal jet. On the way down, Jon told me what had happened, as he understood it from the sheriff in Wyoming."

*"Kris, Sheriff Dugan, out in Cody, says that he doesn't know all the details, but that Joshua has been through hell. And he said that wasn't just a figure of speech. They didn't get all of the people out, and a deputy sheriff helping Joshua was killed. I don't know how Joshua will take it, but this*

*one was different."*

"I knew how Joshua would take it. He would take it hard. But I had no idea how he would handle it. For the first time since San Francisco, I was nervous about seeing him."

*The Learjet lands and taxis over to the private section of the terminal. Jon and Kristian drive in the squad car onto the tarmac and over to the plane. The hatch opens upward and a case of stairs unfolds.*

*The two dogs come down first, barking and wagging and going through their usual happy-to-see-you antics in spite of everything. Joshua is still on board. The sheriff and the woman can see him inside, talking to the pilot. The two men shake hands and Joshua emerges, carrying his duffel in his left hand. He has the look of a man who has lived through a battle....a battle that didn't go well.*

Kristian fell silent. Maureen Andersen prompted her.

"How did he look, Kris? I mean, what was he like? How did he deal with it?"

"I was stunned. I had never seen Joshua like that, not even when I lost the baby. He held me tight and strong, but there was a quiver through his strength that went beyond fatigue. And for the first time I understood how much I meant to him and how much he needed me. I was so ashamed that I cried."

"God, it felt good to hold Kristian again," Joshua remembers. "I didn't know what to say. I wanted to tell her everything, but I couldn't say anything. I kept choking up. I had been gone less than a day, but it seemed like years. There had been times during the past twenty-four hours when I didn't think I would ever see Kristian again. Now, I didn't want to ever let her go. Then I thought about Guy Macauley and his wife."

*The three people and two dogs drive north through the long summer evening, past grazing cows and closing late-summer day lilies. Joshua rides shotgun and looks out the window, still unable to speak. Kristian sits in the back seat, leaning forward behind her husband, her arms around his neck, her head on his shoulder. She has to be careful of his burns. Jonathan VanStavern drives. He wants to say something – but what? He knows his friend is in no mood for a pat on the back, but hell, condolences aren't exactly right either.*

*"Mick Dugan called. He said you and the dogs were absolutely incredible."*

*Joshua turns and looks at his old friend. Jonathan is shocked by what he sees. Joshua starts to speak, then he looks away again at the rolling farms and woods.*

*Yeah, he thinks to himself, we were fuckin' incredible, as the frustration and pain and fear well up inside.*

*Jonathan and Kristian look at each other in the rearview mirror.*

"I remember that ride, Josh. That was one long ride up from Wausau."

Joshua knows what he means. "Sorry about that, Jon, but I was shot clear to hell. I'd been close to forty hours without sleep. Seemed like every time I closed my eyes on that damn plane I would run into Guy Macauley or the fire, or I would feel the cold, dead lips of the people I had failed to save. But that was only part of it. I kept going over the things I had done and the things I could have done, *should* have done, different. And I knew that something had happened during that rescue. Something had changed. I couldn't quite put my finger on it, but it had me worried."

"You did everything you could, Josh, and then some. You know that."

Joshua thinks, *maybe.*

"Kris offered to draw me a bath and do the chores herself. That was nice of her, especially seeing as she didn't look like she was in too great shape herself. But I had some things to do, and I didn't feel much like talking.

"And now as I look back on it, maybe that's where I went wrong."

Kristian has difficulty continuing. Her voice is hushed and tears are welling up. "I remember Josh left his gear on the porch and put up the dogs. Then he started in on the chores. I could see that he was exhausted, but I could also see he was troubled, so I left him alone.

"I went inside and put together a light supper, but Joshua didn't come in until after dark, and even then he just picked at his food.

"He got up and started to put away his gear, and I finally decided that enough was enough."

*She takes his hand and leads him into the darkened bedroom. She starts to unbutton his shirt. She is startled by his burns. Kristian insists that he allow her to bathe and dress his wounds. He does, then follows her lead and watches with aching pleasure as this beautiful woman undresses herself and leads him to their bed.*

*They lie down together. She cuddles into his arms, her head against his chest. She is surprised at how smoky he still smells. She sighs as she feels his arms tighten around her and she passes into exhausted sleep.*

"I awoke sometime in the middle of the night, startled to find Joshua no longer in bed. I got up and put on one of his big flannel shirts that always made me feel so warm and so safe, and I noticed that the light was on in the den.

"Joshua was seated at the hand-crafted cherry wood desk his father had made during the Depression. There was an open bottle of whiskey and a glass on the left side of the desk and several crumpled sheets of paper on the hardwood floor. He was using the old fountain pen he always liked to use for personal letters, but I couldn't imagine who he was writing to at that hour, and I was afraid to ask.

"He kept wiping his eyes with his left hand, and I realized, to my utter astonishment, that he was crying."

"My God, Kris. Look, if all this is too personal...."

Kristian did not hear her.

"I don't know whether he heard me or was just oblivious to me, but he didn't start when I walked up behind him and lightly touched his shoulder."

*"Joshua, what is it?"*

*He finishes the multi-page letter, lays down his pen, and wipes his eyes again.*

*"How does this sound?" he asks, handing her the letter.*

*She reads the letter, written in that long flowing hand of his, to a woman he has never met but whose husband had saved his life and that of a boy. It is one of the most beautiful things Kristian has ever read and she is speechless. She had no idea.*

"That was how I learned a little about what had happened. Joshua never spoke any more about it. He looked up at me but, at the time, all I could do was nod."

"He folded the letter and addressed and sealed the envelope. Then he got up and led me back to our room."

# Chapter Thirty

*He hasn't thought about that game for years. He wasn't thinking about it now – not consciously, at least – but there it was. The fifth game of the season, mid-October of his sophomore year and homecoming to boot. This was the big one, the traditional rivalry between Merrill and Geneva and the one that counted.*

*It didn't matter that, with Joshua Travis starting at left end, Merrill was undefeated and Geneva was only playing fifty-fifty ball. This one game would make or break the season and everyone was up for it – on both sides.*

*Merrill didn't waste any time. Joshua took the opening kickoff and ran it back ninety-seven yards for a touchdown. But Geneva was pumped. They drove eleven plays, more than eighty yards, for a touchdown on their first possession, evening the score.*

*And so it went all night. Merrill, clearly the superior team, opening big holes and connecting for long plays; and Geneva, just as clearly playing above their ability, grinding out yardage, going for it on fourth and three, and never letting Merrill put the game out of reach.*

*Early in the fourth quarter Merrill was up by three. They had the ball on their own forty yard line and were moving well. They should have stayed on the ground, using the threat of a pass only to open up the secondary, but they had been connecting to Joshua all night long and the coach saw no reason to change. But the Geneva coach saw plenty of reason to change, and by then he had his defensive backs double-teaming Joshua.*

*The ball was thrown a little wide, but Josh had it in his hands and was bringing it in. Then it happened. The safety hit him low from behind just as the corner-back drove his helmet into Joshua's chest and knocked him backward. The ball popped out of his hands and was loose.*

*It should have been ruled incomplete. He never had real possession. But the ref didn't see it that way. Neither did the Geneva linebacker who scooped the ball up and ran it all the way back for a TD!*

*The crowd was going wild. Both benches emptied and there surely would have been a brawl had it not been for the fact that Joshua Travis was still lying on the field at the twenty yard line.*

*His father raced out of the stands and onto the field along with the coach, the trainer, and Doc Lieberman. Eventually Joshua was helped to his feet. He was able to leave the field under his own power, more or less, and to the roar of the crowd that he never heard. But he had to sit out the kickoff and the next two possessions, and Geneva, up by four, held.*

*With less than a minute to play and the Jays with the ball, Joshua convinced Coach Dowd, over the objections of Doc Lieberman and the trainer, to put him back in. This time they played it smart. If Joshua was double covered, the ball would be thrown or run to the opposite side of the field. If he was open or covered by only one man, which wasn't often, Joshua would get the ball.*

*The strategy was working but it was eating up valuable time, and it finally came down to just one play. Merrill used its last time out.*

*"I can get open in the far left corner of the end zone," Joshua told the coach and his teammates.*

*"Are you sure?" asked the quarterback, "they're sticking to you like glue."*

*"I'm sure," Josh answered confidently.*

*Coach Dowd hesitated and then nodded. "Do it!"*

*Everyone in the stadium was frantic. The crowd was on its feet. The Geneva coach was going crazy, running up and down the sideline shouting instructions and going with a three man line just like the pros.*

*The quarterback had plenty of time. Joshua charged directly at the safety in the middle of the end zone. Then, as the corner-back raced over to help out, Joshua made his move. Sure enough, he was open in the deep left corner and here came the ball, big and high and fast!*

*Joshua sprang for the ball with all his length and all his athletic ability. He touched the ball with his fingertips ten feet in the air and gave it all he had!*

*When he crashed back down to earth his hands were empty.*

*The next morning was clear and crisp with a heavy frost covering the golden orange dark. His father wasn't surprised to find the morning chores all done by five-thirty. He reckoned that his son would want to be well settled in a tree blind on the edge of the woods by first light. But he was puzzled when he saw his son's boots out in the mud room, and he was amazed to find his son's bow still in place on the rack in the den.*

*Mr. Travis took his steaming coffee outside, walked around to the far side of the sweet corn, and quietly positioned himself in some brush near where he thought he heard a dear rustling.*

*As he peered through the bushes he was absolutely amazed. What he had taken to be a deer in flight was, in fact, his son doing wind sprints up and down a hill in the moonlit dark. On second thought, he wasn't surprised at all.*

*Everyone in Merrill knew that Joshua Travis had played his heart out and that the loss surely wasn't his fault. Everyone knew but Joshua, who didn't quite see it that way. In his eyes he was responsible, and he wasn't about to let it happen again.*

*Every spare moment was spent running or jumping or practicing moves. He carried a football everywhere he went, and he got anyone he could find to throw it to him, even his mother. He hit free weights for the first time, and at night he would fall asleep with playbooks in his hands.*

*His father helped him a lot, while advising him to let up just a little.*

*Telling him that the loss wasn't his fault and to keep things in perspective. Hell, it was only a game.*

*Joshua said he knew. But he didn't let up.*

*That year was the first year since he was eleven – the only year outside some of his service and traveling years – that he didn't get a deer. But that loss to Geneva was Merrill's only loss during the three years that Joshua Paul Travis played varsity ball and that included two state championships.*

"Aldo Leopold wrote a wonderful line," Kristian explained to Maureen, "in his 'November' essay\*, I think. Something about it being warm behind the driftwood because the wind has gone away with the geese. Then he says that he would go too, if he were the wind. I've always loved that line and what happened next always brings it to mind."

Andersen nodded. "Tell me."

"We went back to bed, and I hoped that writing that letter would help Joshua as much as he had intended it to help the woman who had lost her husband."

"The deputy's wife…"

"Yes."

"But it didn't…"

"No, it didn't. At first I thought things might be okay. Joshua fell right asleep. But I guess he still kept a lot on his mind. He tossed and turned all night, flailing through his dreams and his nightmares.

"The day after Josh's return from Cody was Sunday, and I slept a little late. It was raining, and I wasn't surprised to find coffee on the stove and the morning chores all done. I didn't see Joshua, but the pickup was out front, so I knew he was around.

"I thought he might have gone fishing. He liked to do that,

sometimes, when he wanted to be alone, even in the rain, if it wasn't raining too hard. But it was raining cats and dogs that day, and when I saw his fishing rods and tackle box still in the tack room, I knew he wasn't fishing.

"Normally, I wouldn't have given it a second thought, but I knew he was still exhausted, and I was concerned about the way he was taking that damned rescue out in Wyoming. Everyone who knew about it thought Joshua was a real hero. Even that damn board of review finally concluded that everybody did everything right, and that, given the circumstances, it was a near miracle that there wasn't greater loss of life or property. A miracle they rightfully credited to the men and women on the ground.

"But Joshua didn't see it that way. Joshua thought he was responsible for three people's deaths, and I think that was almost too much for him to bear.

"I took my morning coffee out on the porch and sat down to watch the rain and wait for Joshua to return. It was then that I heard the dogs barking off in the distance, on the far side of the alfalfa field."

*She throws on a poncho and picks up her coffee, walking calmly, but warily towards the distant barking. Her sneakers and the legs of her jeans are getting soaked and muddy as she slips and sloshes her way through the fragrant cut and windrowed hay that will have to be raked again. She climbs the rise that separates the hayed field from the fallow one where, at one corner off to the west, she knows are wild raspberries and young white pine.*

*At the edge of the woods she can hear the dogs barking excitedly and making a row and she is frightened. A shudder runs down her spine when she sees him.*

"...and there he was, at seven o'clock on a Sunday morning, with three of the dogs, running tracking problems in the pouring rain!"

"I should have known better," Joshua acknowledged, "so I guess it was my fault mostly, but dammit, Jon, I couldn't get it out of my mind. Any free moment I had would take me back to the fire. Every time I closed my eyes, I would see that girl and her father and Guy Macauley with his head bashed in and burned.

"I went over that damned rescue a thousand times in my head, Jon, but I could never come up with more than two getting out. That should have told me something right there, I reckon. But not an old hammer head like me. I just figured that if I could just get a little bit faster, just get the dogs a little bit sharper, just have better equipment, better communications, better, better...I don't know what, that that would fix everything and keep me from losing any more people..."

"Goes with the territory, Josh, like sheriffing. I've told you that."

"Yes you have, Jon. I've just never really accepted it, and I had sure caught myself in a real pickle. I was scared to death of the next rescue. Each time the phone rang, my heart would stop – and then pound like hell until Kristian or I answered it and realized it wasn't the call – not that time, anyway.

"How the hell had I gotten myself into such a jam? All I ever wanted to do was pull down barns and have a few dogs and a horse or two. And all I wanted was to hold Kristian close and to hunt and fish and hike and eat pie and coffee on rainy days and to have a few kids to play with and to raise.

"And all I could do was work tracking problems and conditioning exercises and think of different ways to do things and new things to try. It didn't matter where I was or what I was doing, search-and-rescue were always lurking somewhere in my mind."

"Things were never the same after Cody," Kristian continued

slowly. She had never confided what had come next to anyone other than Jane. It was difficult for her now. The painful memories always saddened her. Saddened and embarrassed her. "It's hard to say exactly how things changed, but they did. Joshua was still warm and kind and generous, as always, but for the first time he was also aloof and *pressé*, as his relatives would say. It used to be that when I was with Joshua, whether it was for five minutes or five hours, I always felt like I was the only thing in the world that mattered to him. After Cody, that just wasn't so. I always felt like he was somewhere else, or wanted to be somewhere else, and usually he was. He was always working or doing chores or practicing tracking problems or exercising, and he never lingered over things like he used to."

"Lingered?"

"I know that sounds stupid and petty, but his calm, relaxed confidence in everything he did was what made him so great, and now all that was gone.

"I told myself that it would pass with time, hopefully after the next rescue, and that I would just have to be patient and supportive until it did. But it didn't pass, and I used that to justify, in my own mind at least, the decision I had made that night when he was gone. Because what would I do the next time he went off after some lost kids or the time after that, or the time when Joshua would refuse to call it quits even though he knew it was hopeless?"

"Like this last rescue! Oh my God, Kris, now I'm beginning to understand what you must have gone through this weekend. I'm so sorry... If I had only known..."

Kristian hesitated. She wet her lips. "I'd always been determined to make my own life, the one I wanted. I felt sucked in and trapped, and I made up my mind to get out. Thought I was out.... Now I know what scared me so much when I saw *A Man and a Woman* for the first time."

"Of course, the fear of the man you love getting killed," Andersen surmised.

"No, it wasn't just fear of the man I loved getting killed. It was fear of not having a life outside of the man I loved. Does that make any sense?"

Andersen considered the idea for a moment.

"It makes a lot of sense. What did you do?"

Kristian paused and looked across the table at her friend, her eyes moistening again. She took a deep breath and tried to compose herself before continuing. "I went back on the pill. That's what I did. And I didn't tell Joshua."

Andersen considered what Kristian had just told her, then nodded her understanding. "Did he ever find out?"

Kristian thought for a moment. "I don't know. I'm not sure. He never said anything, but it didn't matter. I couldn't lie to Joshua or deceive him, and I couldn't bring myself to tell him, so I did the only other thing I could think of… I left."

*It's a cold, damp November morning on the day he takes Kristian to the Wausau airport. As he loads her bags in the back of the truck, he looks up at the dark gray sky, trying to figure out if it is going to rain or snow.*

"And that's when it hit me, Jon. What a Class A jerk I had been since Cody. Because Kris was looking for the same kind of one hundred percent guarantee about me and us and having kids that I was looking for on rescue operations, and those kinds of guarantees just aren't in the cards, are they? You either play the hand you're dealt, or you get out of the game. And I guess she decided to get out."

"She was scared silly, Josh, and worried."

"I know. I didn't know then but I surely do now. I just wish we had talked things out more. But I guess it took me a long time after Cody to come to my senses.

"I spent the night before she left in the den because Kris had asked me to. She said that if we slept together, she wouldn't be able to leave in the morning. I told her she didn't have to leave, but she said, *yes*, she did.

"Next day, Kristian wouldn't let herself say goodbye to the animals. Said she wouldn't be gone that long, and that it was no big deal. But she didn't fool ol' Jenny-Dog or Jake, who were out roaming around but came in special to nuzzle up to her. That really got to her, especially Jake who, old as he was, normally didn't care a hoot about anything outside of his stomach and his groin, and I could see that Kris was in tears when she climbed into the pickup.

"I had Jenny jump into the back, figuring it might help, but it didn't. Whatever was driving her to leave sure wasn't making her happy.

"As we drove out the drive and turned onto the dirt road, I decided it was going to snow."

*He carries her bags through the cold and the flurries, into the small terminal and helps her check them at the gate. There isn't much time but it's just as well. There's not much left to do or to say.*

*"Do you have enough money?" he asks her.*

*She nods silently.*

*"Don't hesitate to write checks on our account. Hell, more than half of whatever's in there is rightfully yours."*

*"I won't need much," she says softly.*

*"Call me if you need anything – anything at all."*

*Once again she nods, fighting back tears. It's time to go.*

*Now it's his turn to fight back tears.*

*"Do you really have to go?"*

*She nods that she does.*

*"Just for a little while," she lies to herself.*

*"Kristian," he begins, but he doesn't know what to say that will change things and make them better, so he tells her the only thing there is*

*left to say, "I love you."*

*"I know, Joshua," she tells him honestly as she hugs him then turns and hurries up the slippery metal steps to the small twin prop plane waiting to take her to Minneapolis where she will change for San Francisco.*

*He turns and walks back through the cold, wet, gray day to the jeep pickup with the dog in the back. Driving back to Merrill, he tries not to play it over and over again. What's the use? But it's no damn good. All the beauty in his world, in his life, just up and flew away, and it was his own damn, stupid fault. November used to be one of his favorite months. Now it's his worst.*

*Outside of Merrill, he pulls into the Blazer for a drink.*

*"Good to see you, Josh," Patrick tells him. "It's been a long time. How's Kris?"*

*Joshua looks at him and tells him that Kristian has gone to California for the holidays, not wanting to lie but not wanting to talk either. Then he asks Pat to sell him a bottle. Patrick is not supposed to — so he gives him one, on the house, and scratches his head as Joshua leaves.*

*Joshua heads for home, but when he gets there he leaves the engine running and runs into the house just long enough to find his father's old corn-cob pipe and an unopened can of cherry pipe tobacco.*

*He gets back into the pickup and drives northwest a spell, up towards Joe Snow Creek. There, he gets out and changes the hubs. He four wheels it along the two-track as far as he can go.*

*When he can't push the jeep any further he gets out and lets Jenny-Dog out of the back. They hike in and climb up towards the head of the creek.*

*Finally they make it up as high as they can go, to a wooded bluff overlooking the river and the valley below. He squats down against an old oak stump, charges and lights his pipe, and takes a drink from the bottle of Canadian whiskey.*

*It's blowing and snowing pretty good now, but it's not sticking. And anyway, he thinks, what the hell's the difference?*

"I remember putting my arm around Jenny and thinking that she was the only thing I really cared about anymore. Nothing else seemed to matter, and I wondered how things could have changed so much just by someone getting on an airplane and leaving. And I even wondered if I would harvest a deer that year, and I couldn't understand why I didn't care.

"I remember smoking Dad's pipe and drinking the whiskey and stroking Jenny-Dog while we sat and looked out over the brown and gray valley. And I remember thinking that that damn ol' fire out near Cody, Wyoming maybe took more victims than I had figured."

*Kristian Fisk-Travis sits at the table in the tavern, gazing into her friend's moist, blinking eyes.*

*"What will you do now?" the journalist asks*

*Kristian does not have an answer.*

*Joshua Paul Travis looks out through the bright, snowy night, watching the sheriff drive home to his wife.*

*"What will you do if she does come back?" VanStavern had asked before he left.*

*Joshua does not know.*

*He sips his drink and gazes into the fire.*

*High on the Tusayan Plateau, Gogyeng Sowuhti is crying. The Son of Light has survived Masauwu's test of his spirit. She knows that the most difficult trial of all is yet to come.*

# References

*Chapter 30 reference: 'If I Were the Wind' November, Sand County Almanac: and sketches here and there by Aldo Leopold, 1949, 1968.

CPSIA information can be obtained
at www.ICGtesting.com
Printed in the USA
LVHW041024040819
626450LV00039B/1557